"Annie?" Set  and his cell

Instead of head_____nd
to take the long_____ss
the street to a s~~idewalk that kept the ocean in~~ sight.

"I'm fulfilling my obligation to let you know that
I received the results of a pregnancy test a few
minutes ago," she said.

And he knew. The words were professional, but the
tone of her voice...

"You're pregnant," he said.

"Yes." Her tone changed a bit, grew stronger, and he
wondered if his was the first call she'd made. Was
he getting the news almost as soon as she was?

Why that should matter, he couldn't say, but he
couldn't deny the surge of emotion that quickened
his pace for a step or two.

Dear Reader,

Welcome to my 100th published book of love and hope with Harlequin! It's fitting that this book takes place at The Parent Portal—a place where people find hope and believe in miracles. Where science and heart work together to make families. Seth and Annie have broken each other's hearts. But the science they created together years ago can bring them back together. They have work to do. Healing to do. I loved watching their story unfold and I'm excited to share it with you.

I write to entertain you, but also to bring you hope for your own happiness, to build your faith that, ultimately, all will be well and to leave you with an assurance that no matter what today brings, no matter what agonies you might have faced or be facing, love is always there, ready to hold you. I believe in and write about a love that defies science and is more powerful than hate. A love that is a priceless possession that everyone can own and that multiplies within us the more we give it away.

I pray that as you turn the pages you feel the love.

Tara Taylor Quinn

Their Second-Chance Baby

TARA TAYLOR QUINN

HARLEQUIN
SPECIAL
EDITION

ISBN-13: 978-1-335-40481-7

Their Second-Chance Baby

Copyright © 2021 by TTQ Books LLC

This edition published by arrangement with Harlequin Books S.A.

For questions and comments about the quality of this book,
please contact us at CustomerService@Harlequin.com.

Harlequin Enterprises ULC
22 Adelaide St. West, 40th Floor
Toronto, Ontario M5H 4E3, Canada
www.Harlequin.com

Printed in U.S.A.

Having written over ninety novels, **Tara Taylor Quinn** is a *USA TODAY* bestselling author with more than seven million copies sold. She is known for delivering intense, emotional fiction. Tara is a past president of Romance Writers of America and a seven-time RITA® Award finalist. She has also appeared on TV across the country, including *CBS Sunday Morning*. She supports the National Domestic Violence Hotline. If you need help, please contact 1-800-799-7233.

Books by Tara Taylor Quinn

Harlequin Special Edition

The Parent Portal

Having the Soldier's Baby
A Baby Affair
Her Motherhood Wish
A Mother's Secrets
The Child Who Changed Them
Their Second-Chance Baby

The Daycare Chronicles

Her Lost and Found Baby
An Unexpected Christmas Baby
The Baby Arrangement

The Fortunes of Texas

Fortune's Christmas Baby

Visit the Author Profile page
at Harlequin.com for more titles.

To Loriana Sacilotto, Dianne Moggy and Margaret Marbury, who've not only shared the one hundred books' worth of years with me but also given their lives to the greater purpose of putting love, hope and good feeling into the world. Without you, I wouldn't be me.

Chapter One

"Lieutenant, I just…thank you…"

Annie Morgan looked into the tearful eyes of the woman who'd stopped her in a police headquarters hallway and felt her heart lurch strongly.

"Mrs. Milkin." She took Bonnie's outstretched hand. "We're grateful to you for your willingness to come speak so candidly with those on the runaway youth task force. It has to cost you more than I can even imagine, reliving all the stages of losing your son. But I promise you, the insights you've shared, the little signs that so often go unnoticed along the way…you're helping to save lives."

Annie could have added a whole lot more—that

this joint task force encompassed eleven police pro-grams in Southern California, that it was committed to identifying, helping and protecting these chil-dren—but it had all been said, minutes before, in the morning seminar.

She had another appointment to get to in San Diego that August morning. One she was anticipat-ing with great dread. And hope. It wouldn't be easy, seeing her ex-husband for the first time in ten years. But the end result...

But appointment aside, she'd take time for Bon-nie. Running fingers through her short blond hair, she said, "Your dedication to your son, evident in all the ways you tried to intervene, all the various areas of help you sought on his behalf, your constant, unconditional love in the face of an addiction that wouldn't let go of him, even this today, honoring his legacy after his death by helping others in his situ-ation... These are all examples to me of the kind of parent I want to be..."

"You don't have children, then?" Bonnie asked, starting slowly toward the elevator again. Annie's stomach reacted to the question. Jumped and flipped. Slipping into the white cardigan sweater she'd worn into work with black dress pants, and a black tank shirt, adjusting the sweater to cover the gun at her waist, Annie kept step with Bonnie.

"Not yet," she answered. Not yet, but...soon?

"I'm surprised," Bonnie said. "You're so...nurturing."

Annie glanced over at her again. As a cop—first in the military, then working up to detective in Los Angeles, and finally to lieutenant in the smaller Marie Cove community—Annie had been called many things, but couldn't recall "nurturing" being among them. She cared. She just showed it in different ways.

Before she'd turned to police work, had her heart broken, and her faith shaken in a way she'd never thought it could be, maybe she'd been...nurturing. After all, she'd once thought that her life's purpose was first and foremost to be a parent.

"I'm...actually on my way to a meeting regarding in vitro implantation," she suddenly confided. That was something that no one but her doctor and the employees at The Parent Portal knew. But Bonnie had just laid her heart bare to a roomful of strangers. She'd talked about her own struggle to have a child. And about how she now lived for other people's children, wanting to do all she could to help them. Her openness had brought a rawness to the situation that seemed to call for the same from others. "And there's no cause to worry," Annie inserted quickly. "I spearheaded this task force, but there are many others who are as committed to its success as I am."

"I wasn't worried," Bonnie said. "You're entitled to your own life, Lieutenant."

Annie was a bit stunned by Bonnie's astuteness, by the fact that Bonnie seemed to understand that, while Annie felt she was on the right track, personally, she still felt guilty in terms of the job she'd put first for so long. But before she could say anything, Bonnie continued on. "Are you being implanted here in San Diego? This morning?" Her eyes lit up with joy in spite of her own sad ending.

Annie shook her head. "No, just checking on the embryos."

"Well, just in case you're wondering, I'd do it all over again in a heartbeat," Bonnie said. "My boy, he had his challenges, and his life was far too short, but the love he brought to my world...it was real and deep and lives inside me every day. There's nothing like it."

There was nothing like it. That's what she knew. What her heart had been telling her. She'd wanted so many things out of life, but being a parent had been absolutely top of the list. And with all of the seedy side she saw of life, she wanted to be a part of the healthy and happy and good parts, too. Because she knew they existed. In greater numbers than the bad.

Her plan was healthy. She had no reason to feel guilty. And yet, as the elevator door binged, her stomach lurched again. She was going to see Seth. The man she'd once thought was the other half of her soul. Someone she'd trusted implicitly to have her back. Someone for whom she'd gladly postponed her own advancement. She'd been a bit off her game that morning, coming close to having to pull off the freeway and collect herself during the drive down to San Diego from Marie Cove. Work had taken her out of her own anxieties and then, as soon as the seminar had ended, tension had besieged her once again.

And before panic could take root, weaken her, Bonnie Milkin had been there, giving her a positive response to her having a child of her own. Exactly what she'd needed to hear.

A stranger who'd had no way of knowing…

There couldn't be a mistake about that.

The universe had given her a sign that she was on the right course.

Seth had no reason to deny her. She wasn't asking for anything *he* wanted. His okay and a signature— were all it would cost him.

Pressing her brown leather satchel tightly against her side, she moved forward with the rest of the people entering the elevator doors. Inside was the paperwork that, once signed and notarized, would allow her to finally start a family of her own.

She'd faced down murderers and won. No way a little thing like a signature was going to scare her off.

And seeing Seth again?

Well, that was no more than just part of the job at hand. Like facing the internal affairs bureau at work after a good shoot. You didn't like it. You did it. You got through it.

And doing so allowed you to live the life you loved.

Judge Advocate General attorney Seth Morgan knew he was powerful enough, strong enough to have faced hardened criminals, and fought and won intricate and powerful battles in courts all over the world. But on that August day, he felt more like the unassuming, blond-haired, blue-eyed nice guy his appearance made him out to be.

In his white navy uniform, everything about him as pristine as it had ever been, he could do no more to prepare for the event ahead than tend to his appearance. He had absolutely no idea what the upcoming meeting with his first ex-wife could be about. They'd split amicably ten years before. Had emailed on occasion, through the years, as some piece of paperwork or whatnot had warranted. He'd written to tell her he was getting remarried seven years before. Had seemed the decent thing to do when sitting alone late one night, wistfully remembering his first wedding. She'd written a note of sympathy when, two years later, he'd sent an email telling her that that marriage had also failed.

But though they'd lived just an hour and a half apart for much of the past decade, neither had ever reached out for any physical contact. So why would she want to see him now?

Could be she was working a case with a sailor involved. He worked military justice. One of his guys could have gotten into trouble up in Marie Cove. Not a stretch to think that navy sailors would choose to spend off time in the small, elite beach community, with its upscale dining and entertainment choices and without the touristy crowds.

If she'd had a case, an email, or—worst-case scenario—a phone call, would have sufficed. At least initially.

He didn't like going into meetings cold. Without an ability to prepare responses.

How could he plan for the meeting's success without knowing the other side's goal? Or complaint?

Without knowing the charges?

Clearly, something was wrong. No way Annie would just stop by because she was in the area.

Adjusting the computer screen fixed to his desk, moving the mounting arm and tilting the screen, he sat back. Looked at the news page that was on his monitor and moved both pieces of the apparatus back to their original positioning.

Maybe she was getting married. His gut tightened at the thought. At the reminder of how bad he'd been at that age-old institution. Twice. And, okay, he felt some twinges at the thought of another man being able to give her what he could not. But he wanted her to be happy. They wanted each other's happiness. Hence the divorce.

He quickly dismissed the marriage possibility, anyway. She'd send the announcement by email, if she bothered to inform him at all.

Fifteen minutes before they were due to meet, he left base to head to the small office he'd been allotted at the local community center where he helped the homeless pro bono.

The office—private for the sake of clients who might not come to see him otherwise—was kept locked, and he opened it up. He turned on the overhead light and ran a cloth over the scarred pressboard table and leatherlike orange couch that took up the side wall opposite his desk. The place was professionally cleaned at the end of each day he was there, but still, this was *Annie*.

The woman he'd once believed to his core was the love of his life.

Annie, whom he hadn't seen in ten years…other than the odd photo or two he'd looked up on the internet during this or that long night of wakeful memories over the years. If she was on social media, her accounts were private. But there'd been the photo of her with the Marie Cove chief of police when she'd been made lieutenant of the detective squad there a couple of years before. And earlier ones—her among the other twelve members of her police academy graduation class. A headshot when she made detective in LA.

She'd been twenty-eight the last time he'd seen her, thirty-six in the most recent photo, and the shock that had splintered through him as she looked out at him from that generic capturing of her smile had never completely subsided. It had always been that way with them. Her tall, lithe, athletic body, only four inches shorter than his six feet, had been flame to his match from the first day they'd met.

The knock on the door stopped his world for a split second. Leaning over the bottom drawer of his desk, about to stash away the cloth he'd used, he just froze. Staring at the door. One of the reasons he'd been given the office was that it was the only room attached to the community center with an outside, private entrance.

And the one that he'd instructed Annie to use in his last email to her, confirming their meeting.

The distance between his desk and the door perpendicular to it was minimal. He took each step slowly, feeling rushed.

Unprepared.

Like a tornado lurked overhead, ready to touch down. The power. The awe. The otherworldliness. The loss of control.

The devastation it could cause.

The fear.

Where he'd once believed the sun would shine forever.

Yeah. It was all coming back to him.

* * *

It seemed to take forever for the door to open. Standing there in the warmth of August sunshine, Annie knew it was probably only seconds before she heard the turn of the latch, but the eternity stretched on as she looked toward the opening. Starved for a sight of the man she'd loved with every aspect of her being.

She'd done great things in her life without him.

Didn't regret her choices where he was concerned. How could she? Those had been the right ones.

And yet…

For a second, as he stood there in his dress whites, she catapulted back to being a new navy recruit meeting him for the first time. Pulled into a world of slow motion where his short blond hair was all she saw. And then those blue eyes sucked her in until she was floundering in a massive pool of longing. Of sorrow.

Of need.

Of knowing *him*.

"Seth." She spoke first. It was right. She'd asked for the meeting.

"Annie, come in." His tone, his manner…were all top-notch. Professional with a touch of easy familiarity. As if they'd passed in the hall on a regular basis. If he was at all moved by the sight of her, he hid the feelings well.

A bit more confident in her mission, she entered

his domain. And stopped the second she got a look at the mostly bare, sterile and unimaginative room. Utility-style, professional-grade, gray linoleum floors. Clean plaster walls, white paint that appeared to have yellowed with age, and zero decor. A scarred desk, not unlike something the department had donated after finding it in the station house basement the year before. A couch from a bygone era—she'd seen one like it in a crack house, once, though Seth's was in much better shape. What passed as a coffee table. It had four legs and a top.

"What is this place?" She'd looked up the address the second he'd sent it to her. Meeting at a community center had seemed smart, considering that she hadn't wanted to be trapped at a table with wait service interruptions, and, due to regulations, couldn't get on base to see him. She'd expected a conference room.

"My office."

"Your...what?" Confused, she frowned at him, raised a hand to brush at her hair and felt her gun against her elbow as her arm dropped heavily back to her side.

She needed to sit down. To breathe through the jitters that were attacking her insides. To put some distance between them. His nearness... How could ten years not change the scent of a man? Had to be the cologne. Though his brand was no longer being made—she'd had a moment when she'd read that the company was going under. He'd found some musky companion to it, apparently.

The tiny room didn't allow the amount of space she needed.

"I volunteer here some evenings and weekends," he said. "This room is reserved solely for my purpose. Gives clients a modicum of privacy and ensures that my supplies are where I need them when I need them. And the perk of sole use is probably a sign of gratitude, too."

The tenor of his voice…it gave her shivers. The good kind.

No. Not good.

Nothing about her intense reaction to Seth Morgan could in any way be considered good. She had to state her business, make a request, arrange for signatures and depart.

As soon as possible.

In her world, the literal meaning of those words generally came with every second mattering.

"I need your signature on a document," she said, holding her satchel close to her side, as though it contained the biological matter that represented her entire future, rather than just the paperwork that allowed her sole ownership and use of it.

As though she had to protect it from him.

Where before she wanted to sit, she was suddenly glad she was standing, meeting him eye to eye rather than having him tower over her. Yet, when her leg came in contact with the hideous orange-colored, faux leather couch, she sank down to it as though it was her only lifeline.

Seth sat, too, behind his desk. He was frowning. "It's been ten years. What did we miss?"

It wasn't a *miss*. It had just been a dormant possibility, hanging out into infinity.

"And why didn't you just email it to me?" He posed the second question before giving her time to respond to the first. His arms crossed, he sat there with shoulders back, staring her down.

Defensive posturing. Her brain kicked in where emotions were stifling her usual productivity.

She was a listener first. And then a talker. One who sought to understand before attempting to be understood. It made her one of the most respected and well-known interrogators in Southern California law enforcement circles.

"Because it doesn't have to be signed," she said, hoping she was reading his body language well enough to get through to him. "This is more of a request, not a requirement."

When the arms didn't drop, she softened her tone more. "I've come to ask a favor, Seth."

She'd told herself the way to get the job done was to be confident, composed, calm and sure. Not to beg.

She'd been in the room less than two minutes and he'd reduced her to feeling desperate. Or she'd sunk to it on her own. In that moment, she couldn't be sure how much of what was going on was on her or him. The fact that she wanted to be on him…on top of him, out of uniform, moving her body over his…

Oh, God. What if she'd made a horrible mistake, thinking she could handle seeing him?

There'd been a reason they'd stayed away from each other for a decade. *Good* reason.

Apart, they were at the top of their fields. Running exemplary, respectable, successful lives.

Together…they tore at what made each of them their best self.

"State your favor." His tone held no conciliation. Or even a note to signify that they'd known each other once—let alone been deeply, intimately intertwined.

She was losing him. And couldn't let her future just slip away.

Not again.

"I'm sorry," she said, trying for a surface smile that she knew was a total fail. And pushed forward through it. Honesty was the only way… "I'm having a moment here. And I apologize. I didn't expect… it's just, seeing you again…" She inhaled deeply, released the breath slowly. And then again with more haste. If she wasn't careful, she was going to do something supremely immature, like hyperventilate. Forcing herself to hold his still, as-yet unrelenting gaze, she said, "Can we just talk for a minute or two? Just…take a breath?"

Or catch her breath.

Spreading his hands, he didn't even seem to consider her request before spitting a reply. "It's been ten years, Annie. What have we got to talk about?"

She watched those big, capable hands of his drop to his desk. Not return to their nesting places hidden in crossed arms. An opening she welcomed with her whole being.

"This room," she said. "You being here. Tell me about the work you do. Just give us a second to let the energy level subside for a second or two."

When he started to talk, telling her about the people who came to him in that dingy room—a lot of homeless teenagers, among others, seeking assistance with misdemeanor crimes they couldn't afford to defend—and talked about the grant programs he'd found that he could help them maneuver through to better themselves, Annie took her first normal breath. And then another. She listened.

And then *she* talked. Telling him about the runaway youth task force she spearheaded, about the meeting they'd held that morning, her professional reason for being in San Diego, and in so doing, found a piece of herself again.

"Our goal is to help these kids, not wait until we have to arrest them," she said, her mind spinning as she looked at him sitting so forcefully, intentionally behind that ragged desk. "If you'd be willing, I'd love to put you in touch with Captain Ben Kinder, here in San Diego County, who's on the task force. Maybe, with the kids you see here…and our efforts…some greater good could be done…"

His focused nod as he pulled out a notepad and pen to take down Ben's information gave her the first real hope that Seth Morgan, the man she'd once known and adored, might still linger within bits and pieces of the decorated JAG attorney occupying the room with her.

Chapter Two

"I'm surprised that with all of your responsibilities on the base, you have time to spend here at the center," Annie said. Seth absorbed Annie's interest like a man dying of thirst would inhale water.

There'd always been something about her...the way she made him feel like she cared about every single feeling and experience he'd ever had...like she cared about outcomes, not just moments...

"My commission, while requiring much of me, doesn't take up the time that others allot to home and family." Shaking his head as he dropped his pen, he gave what he'd intended to be a flippant response to a question that had turned their conversation personal on a dime.

The second he saw a stricken look cross her features, and then just as rapidly disappear, he shoved his brain into gear. "The truth is, at forty, I've realized that I'm not the family man I thought I wanted to be," he told her. "I'm not good at delivering the goods to the same person, being there for them on a daily basis, being able to tend to the relationship every single day. Some nights, I just need to go home and vegetate quietly." Which she knew all too well.

He didn't put the self-discoveries into words often. Actually never. But if there was one person who deserved to know the results of his years of self-honesty and taking accountability, it was Annie.

"You know that the failures we suffered weren't about you." At the time, he'd sure been willing to blame them on her. The way he'd seen it back then, if she'd only agreed not to pursue her need to be a cop, and find some other dream instead, he'd have given his life to support her on it.

Assuming that her next pursuits didn't also put her life in danger on a daily basis. He'd been wrong to ask her to give up her dream. But right or wrong didn't change the fact that he'd been unable to take on a cop wife.

"I know." Her quiet answer came after seconds of silence.

As she sat there, watching him, he couldn't decipher a single one of her thoughts. But, God, she was beautiful. The black pants and top, the white cardi-

gan, weren't particularly flattering. Nor did they out-
line her still athletic form in any obvious way. And
yet…he'd take her to bed in a second if she'd have
him…and if they didn't have a history.

Seeing her again hadn't embellished his memories
of how hot she was. Or how quickly she got him from
guy in a chair in a room, to a guy who was hard and
aching for sex. The fact that she could still have that
effect on him, while just sitting there, all lieutenant-
like, with that gun at her waist…

Damn.

He'd known attending the meeting without a pre-
stated agenda, without preparation, without expected
goals and outcomes, hadn't been a good plan.

So…he had to come up with one. On the spot. Immediately. It wasn't the first time he'd been required
to do so or managed to successfully do so: he'd done
it more than once, with national security on the line.
He was good at his job. Maybe even great at it.

Which was why he spent most of his free time volunteering those very same services. Kept him from
screwing up in other, less skilled areas of his life.

And hurting people in the process. Himself included.

But Annie, most of all. Working in a different
command, she'd supported him, even putting her
own life plans on hold to re-up for another four years
of duty while he went through law school. And when
it had been time for her turn to pursue her own goals,

his attempt to support her in her endeavor had been a complete fail. Instead, he'd done all he could to get her to change her plans. To be someone he needed her to be, rather than supporting her in living her best life.

She hadn't said a word in a few minutes. Just sat there, looking like she cared, but giving no clue what about.

The meeting needed to move forward.

So…he sat up. Literally and figuratively.

He now knew the agenda. She needed a favor.

And the plan? Grant it, whatever she needed.

"What's this favor you need to ask?"

Annie was grateful to Seth for bringing them back from the precipice. For breaking the silence that had fallen between them at his unusual personal disclosure.

While, on the one hand, she was relieved to hear that he was at peace without having a family, that he'd have no personal use for the embryos she wanted so desperately for herself, she'd been speechless with sadness for him.

What had happened to the man she'd fallen for so completely back when she'd been a new navy recruit?

Had she ever really known Seth Morgan? Had it all been fake?

Needing to know even after all those years, she

said, instead, "I want you to sign an agreement giving me full rights to shared biological material."

Her focus had to be on the future, not the past.

He'd said back then, when their marriage had been falling apart and she'd put him on the spot, that while he'd met a woman who was in his thoughts, he'd never been unfaithful to Annie or their marriage. But had that been the truth?

His frown brought knots to her stomach, and all thoughts of the past fled. They were insignificant mind traps rearing only to distract her from the utmost importance of the matter at hand.

Dear God, don't let him have a problem with her request. Those embryos they'd harvested and fertilized years ago were her only hope now.

And since…

"It's not like you have any use for them." She spoke the noticeably defensive words aloud, all of her often-sought-after interrogation skills, her high level of communication prowess—her ability to understand first, and therefore get her subject to see things clearly—apparently on leave.

She knew she'd made a mistake even before he started shaking his head. And couldn't just offer him a drink, or change the subject again, for a breather.

"Biological matter?" he asked, sounding confused as his frown deepened.

Encouraged by the lack of anger in his tone, she took heart that all might not be lost. It wasn't too late to salvage the conversation and guide it to a more positive end.

But she looked in his eyes…and floundered again, as she swore to herself that she'd seen a glimpse of the Seth Morgan of her dreams. The man she'd lived side by side with for a number of years. She couldn't have made him up and have had a successful relationship with him for nearly ten years. He couldn't have faked his attentiveness, his devotion, for that long.

The intense love she'd once felt for that man couldn't still be hanging out inside her, could it?

She'd known the meeting was going to be hard. She'd had no idea it would be so excruciating.

"The…embryos." The word crackled in the room like a cluster of exploding firecrackers. It fell with a burning sharpness, a deafening noise, and continued to reverberate with the pain of lost dreams after she'd spoken it.

They'd both been so certain…so determined… that their dream of having a family together would happen. And maybe…if she'd been implanted before that last tour rather than choosing to wait until after her deployment…

And in most of the crimes she'd worked on over the years, there'd been that "if": the one turning point that changed an entire life. The defining moment, if only he or she hadn't made that one choice that put them in the perp's life, or vicinity, at the time of the crime…

It took her a second to realize that Seth's expression had changed from perplexed to…stony. A look she knew, one he had rarely turned on her during their years together. Seth, when he was angry, was intimidating at the very least. But he didn't yell. Lash out. Hit.

He turned to stone. Seemed to have his most acute thinking moments encased in that cement. And to lose all ability to feel, too.

But…why would…

"The embryos," he stated. No question, just… repetition.

She nodded anyway. "You're angry."

"Hell, yes, I'm angry."

She'd been very aware of the possibility that Seth might not want her to bring his children into the world after their divorce, but she hadn't figured out-and-out anger. At the very least, she'd expected he'd ask questions before reacting. To find out her plans. No one was bigger on knowing everyone's plans for everything than her ex.

Maybe he was mad that she hadn't offered to share the embryos. Would he prefer that she share them with him? If, deep inside, he still thought he might want children of his own someday, with a woman who couldn't have them for him…he might need them. But there was no telling how many she'd need to conceive even one child…and…

He could always find another surrogate for his sperm.

She couldn't find another man to fertilize her eggs. She was no longer capable of producing a healthy embryo.

Help him understand. The idea came to her. Maybe out of desperation. Maybe because she was always trying to understand others. Conflict resolution was one of her specialties, one of the many things she'd learned about herself on that last tour with the navy.

"Some of my eggs are showing signs of age—premature chromosomal abnormality," she said, pretending she was on the right side of the table in an interrogation room. Trying to hide behind that barrier. "It's quite common in women in their forties, but shocking to me at my age. I just had them tested out of an abundance of caution. I can't start out fresh, Seth. Not without significant risk of birth defect." Whereas his sperm could be good, even when he was an elderly man with great-grandchildren.

His chair hit the wall behind him as he pushed back from the desk. It didn't have far to go—maybe a foot. The room was that small. And with him standing, and her still seated, he seemed to tower over the entire space.

"You're talking about our embryos," he bit out,

arms folded again as he rested his butt against the corner of the old desk. For a second, she thought about his dress whites. About the very good possibility that the desk would leave dirt marks. When her gaze lifted, his bore into hers.

"Yes," she told him, frowning now. He'd seemed perfectly lucid when she'd first come in. Had allowed what was meant to be innocuous conversation, participated generously in it, at her request.

"*Our embryos*." He quietly practically spat the words. "The ones we created together more than a decade ago."

"Yes." What other embryos were there?

His gaze darkened, narrowed, as he jutted his chin. Moisture seemed to be gathering at the corners of his eyes. Or maybe with that chin jut he'd tilted his head up and the light was shining on him differently, giving the illusion that he might be experiencing more emotion than usual.

Her daily work required that she notice such things. Nothing she'd ever done, though, had prepared her for this particular confrontation.

She engaged his stare, giving him as good as he gave, until he brought his fist down to the desk with more force than was kind. And returned to his seat behind the desk.

Seth wasn't a violent man. Even after all that had passed between them, she still believed that much about him was true.

"You're telling me that those embryos still exist?" His words were calm, but issued with a coldness she didn't recognize.

"I'm here. Asking for your signature to release their ownership to me," she stated the obvious. "I have an appointment to be implanted on Saturday."

"How *could* you?" The raised volume didn't cut into her as much as his tone, which continued to be cold.

"How could I what?" Have herself implanted? Have a baby without him? Or without a husband?

"Keep them."

Raising both hands, then letting them fall, she reminded herself of her inner strength, with an elbow touch to her gun. She was a cop who'd taken down fiends. She could fight Seth for a petri dish of microscopic hope.

"You act as if I confiscated them and locked them up in a safe in my closet," she said. "I didn't keep them anymore than you did, Seth. They're right where we left them, stored in the same facility. I haven't done anything but pay the storage bill all these years." It was like she'd walked into some kind of twilight zone.

"Yes, that!" he said, pointing his finger at her as he stood up again. Paced to the outside door and back. "You knowingly kept them. You paid the facility's storage fee."

She didn't get him. Panic rose up inside her. And still, it was good to be in the same room with the man.

Something about him had always had a way of reaching inside her and leaving warmth.

"They sent me a bill, Seth. I sent you a copy. If you'd wanted to pay it, you were more than welcome."

"I didn't want either of us to pay it," he said, turning on his way back to his desk to face her. Looking up at him hurt her neck. Having him stand over her hurt her psyche. She stood, too.

"The bill was in my name. There would have been repercussions to my credit if I hadn't paid it." Even as she said the words, she recognized the inanity of the conversation. Tried to figure out what was really upsetting him, because she knew darn well that no matter how much life might have changed this man, he didn't care that much about a storage bill.

"Not if you'd had them destroyed there wouldn't have been," he said now, face-to-face with her over the two feet that separated them.

"I couldn't destroy them without your permission," she told him. He was a lawyer. He'd know that.

"You couldn't use them without my permission," he told her. "But either one of us had the right to have them destroyed."

And he'd just talked himself into a corner. She knew he knew it. Saw the second that a bit of the wind left his sails.

"You didn't have them destroyed, Seth."

"You always handled all of the appointments and the insurance information..."

Yeah, she'd done everything but put his specimen in a cup for him. Because having their family had meant that much to her. She'd thought he'd needed and wanted her children as badly as she'd wanted his. He'd been in law school when those embryos had been created. She'd upped for another tour doing office work on base until he finished the grueling study and classroom hours required to graduate at the top of his class. She'd been handling most of the household stuff as a result and paying the bills, too. She'd thought that taking care of these insemination details was just more of her carrying the weight for both of them until he was out of school. Then, it would be her turn for college.

At twenty-six, planning to leave the navy, having the baby before she started school had been her idea, so that she didn't have to take maternity leave from her studies. And he'd seemed so on board. Excited, even...

"It never occurred to me that you wouldn't have disposed of them. It was a no-brainer. The marriage was over. Our lives together were over..."

He wasn't just pissed that she was asking to use their embryos. He was angry that they still existed at all. Not something she'd figured into her own reasoning.

"Why didn't you have them destroyed?" His tone softened as he sank back onto the edge of the desk, leaving her standing all alone.

Something she'd learned how to do well in the ten years since the demise of their marriage.

"I don't know," she told him, giving him the total honesty the situation required. "For one thing, I thought I had to contact you to get permission to do it and I didn't want to go there. I figured that if you didn't want to tackle the subject, I'd just leave it alone."

"So…what? You were just going to pay to store them for the rest of your life?"

She shook her head. "I don't know, Seth. I didn't have any far-reaching plans. I just had the bill automatically paid from my account every month and never thought about it. I didn't even think about using them when I made the choice to have a family on my own. Didn't even dawn on me. I was going to use an anonymous sperm donor from The Parent Portal. And then tests came back showing a high risk of possible birth defects. That apparently happens with age. And while I was still reeling from that news, I saw the money pull from the storage facility, for storing healthy embryos made from my eggs, and… here I am."

At his mercy.

And she'd learned a long time ago just how little

she could count on Seth Morgan for his support of her endeavors.

Thinking he'd do this for her…seeing him again at all…had been a big mistake.

"I want no part of any of this."

"I'm not asking you to be a part of it. I just want you to sign a form and I'm out of your life forever."

"You might be, but I'd still have a child walking around out there…"

Her chest tight, she just stood there, with nothing. She'd known, deep in her heart, that it was a longshot. The man she'd known…he wouldn't just blithely sign away a life. She'd convinced herself that man she'd thought she'd known had been a figment of her imagination. Convinced herself her ex-husband lawyer wouldn't care that he had a fatherless child.

"I'm sorry, Annie, but I'm not signing the embryos over to you. I can't." She had her answer.

Wasn't ready to accept it. Might never be ready. But there was no point in remaining with Seth for another second. Because she wouldn't ask any man to sign away a life if it wasn't right for him.

And it wasn't Seth's fault she'd waited so long to start her own family.

Without another word, she walked across the room and let herself out.

He did nothing to stop her.

Didn't even say goodbye.

For the second time in her life, Seth Morgan had quashed her hope.

Chapter Three

He owed her.

He'd been an ass, and he owed her.

She was asking the impossible. She wanted him—a man who'd lost his mother, a law enforcement officer, on the job when he'd been just seventeen—to put his biological child at risk of experiencing that same crushing blow.

He'd still been an ass.

So, what was he saying?

He couldn't help not wanting to go that route himself—being married to someone who put her life on the line every day. He wasn't a guy who just sat back and waited while a loved one was in danger.

But did he have the right to make this decision for a child? For Annie?

Because he knew firsthand what it felt like to have a lieutenant come to his door with that grim look on his face. They hadn't told him that his mother had been killed. He'd only been in high school and it wasn't their place. But as soon as he'd seen their faces, he'd known it must be bad. And when they'd said they were taking him to his father, who was waiting for him at the hospital, he'd known it was his mother who'd fallen.

Still, he'd lived with his father being a cop. Yeah, he wanted the old man to retire, but at sixty-one his dad still wasn't ready yet. Seth didn't like it, but he wasn't losing sleep over it, either. His dad had always been a cop. It was just something he accepted—but he hadn't lost his father in the line of fire.

And then there was Annie…she'd thought she wanted to be some kind of social worker when they'd met, had joined the navy just for the college opportunity. Had never planned to live out her life in harm's way. And for the first few years after they'd married, she hadn't ever wavered from that plan. He'd never have started a relationship with her if he'd known that she might be deployed to an assignment that involved police action, that she'd be offered military police training, or that she'd find her passion within law enforcement.

He'd done his best to accept her calling. To live with it.

He'd failed. Their marriage had suffered.

Deteriorated.

Ended.

And now, a decade later, after he'd created an entirely different, and wholly satisfying, life for himself, she'd come back to disrupt it all again?

As Seth drove back across town to the naval base, getting closer, with every mile, to the ocean he loved, he got angry all over again. He'd long ago made peace with the fact that he wouldn't have the children he'd thought he needed in his life. Had come to see that change as for the best. His job completed him. And took all of him.

His purpose wasn't to put more people in the world, but to help those who were already there and heading down a wrong path.

And then he'd found out that the potential people he and Annie had created all those years ago still existed? And that she wanted to bring at least one of them to life?

No!

Stopping at a light, he caught a glimpse of the ocean in the distance…and clicked into rational mode. Clamped down on emotions that served no good purpose.

It wasn't unreasonable for him to be shocked, upset and opposed to the idea of children he'd wanted to create a decade ago suddenly being born. A possibility he'd thought forever destroyed.

It wasn't fair for him to have just assumed that Annie would have taken care of seeing that those embryos were destroyed. Nor was it right for him to be angry that she hadn't done it. Not when he hadn't done anything to take care of it himself. He hadn't even bothered to check on them.

Shaking his head, he tapped his thumb on the steering wheel. Over and over. Harder and harder. It had just never occurred to him that there'd be a need to follow up on the destruction of their dream after the marriage had imploded.

And the rest of it… Annie's driving down to see him…her reason…

She'd always wanted to grow a baby inside her like no other woman he'd ever known. She used to talk about the desire to feel a little body moving inside her, about the magnitude and responsibility of her ability to take active part in such a miracle. All those months they'd tried to get pregnant naturally, so many times he'd wake up in the middle of the night to find her wide-awake, worrying. He could remember holding her tight as she talked to him about her feelings.

The light changed and he inched forward behind the traffic in front of him.

He wanted her to have her baby. For however long she managed to stay alive and in her child's life, she'd be a great mother. There'd never been a doubt about that.

But *his* child?

He shook his head again as he joined the queue to enter the base.

No way she was having his child.

Not that she wanted him involved in her baby's life. Him happening to be the sperm donor was really a superfluous detail to her.

She wasn't asking him to be a father. She just wanted full ownership of a biological component that contained his contribution.

His temper settled a bit when he thought of it that way. Seth parked his sporty BMW in the covered spot reserved for him and exited out into the warm August air bearing the unique tinge of salt that spoke of home to him. Comfortable in its familiarity.

He said hello to a few people he knew as he entered the building and walked the hallways en route to his office. He felt his phone vibrate with a text. Pulled it from his front pocket.

I've given permission to have the embryos destroyed. The facility is just waiting on you to confirm.

There followed contact information, both online and phone. Name included.

And nothing else.

It didn't surprise him at all that she'd acted so

quickly. That was Annie. Take care of business immediately. Don't let it hang out there, taunting you with hope. As soon as she'd realized that he wasn't okay with her being a cop, she'd been done with the marriage, too. Which was one of the reasons he'd been so shocked to find that she hadn't destroyed those embryos.

In his office, he shut the door behind him. Dropped the phone on his desk. Clicked on the computer screen. Called up the web address she'd typed.

She hadn't asked him to let her know when it was done.

Perhaps she'd already made arrangements to have the facility let her know.

Perhaps she'd already moved on. She was good at that. Moving on. Had certainly moved on from their marriage quickly enough, when he'd indicated that he needed to be through. There'd been no tearful recriminations. No begging him to hang on, to try harder.

No suggestions that she might try to find another career that fulfilled her equally.

No, she'd finished her tour of duty, left the navy as planned, and enrolled in a criminal justice program.

And there she was again, taking care of business before she could possibly have even made it back to Marie Cove.

A vision of those big blue eyes, staring him down less than half an hour before, filled his mind's eye.

Filled him until he could almost feel her presence right there in a room she'd never occupied. But the gaze wasn't defiant as it had been in that stark little room in the community center. Those eyes were slowly welling with tears, tears that she'd fight for all she was worth.

As memory flooded, he knew that sometimes she won that always hard-fought battle. Her will against her tears.

And sometimes she lost.

He'd bet she was crying. Alone somewhere.

When they'd been together, her crying had nearly brought him to tears a time or two. Especially that time when she'd been late and they'd been certain she was pregnant, only to have her start her period in the middle of the night...

He hated it when she cried.

He'd just killed any hope of her realizing her lifelong dream.

Any hope of her giving birth to her own child.

Just as, a decade before, his inability to accept her in a dangerous career had destroyed her dream of being his wife for the rest of their lives.

He had every right to his feelings. Every right to want those embryos destroyed.

Looking at the screen, he typed. Printed. Went out to a paralegal he trusted, to have his signature notarized, and followed it with a quick and deliberate trip to the fax machine.

And then picking up his phone, he typed some more. Hit Send.

And felt sick to his stomach.

Annie felt a text vibrate from the phone in her pants pocket. Ignored it. In her serviceable black work shoes, she was walking along a stretch of beach just north of San Diego. One known to and generally used by locals. The beach she and Seth had used to live by.

Having shed her cardigan and left it in the department sedan she'd been assigned upon making lieutenant, she preferred to focus on the sun flooding her shoulders, rather than any message anyone had sent her.

Sunshine and shoulders. There'd been a song about that. About how sunshine made you happy. It had been written before she was born, but her mom had loved it and played it often. Annie hummed some of the tune, determined to make true the song's message. Wishing her mother was still alive. Chelsea Whitaker Bolin, daughter of the uber-wealthy Claude Charles Whitaker, had died in a boating accident five years before, and Annie still missed her every single day. She'd only been three when her dad, Danny Bolin, had been killed during a robbery at the bank where he worked as a security guard. She'd heard a lot about the man from her mother, but her own memories were vague at best.

Her close relationship with her mother had been part of the reason she'd been so adamant about having a family of her own—even once it became apparent that she'd be doing it solo.

Wiping tears from her face, she skirted clear of a man and little boy up a little farther in the sand, feeling out of place dressed as she was, but unable to leave the beach. There was nowhere else she could think of to go, to get through the devastating pain coursing through her in waves. Over and over. She had friends she could call, of course. And Christine, the owner and manager of The Parent Portal, knew where she was and what she'd hoped to accomplish that day. She had a tentative appointment for implantation scheduled later in the week. Saturday. Three days away. She needed to cancel it.

There was no point in keeping it. It wasn't like she could simply choose a sperm donor and continue on her path. Her eggs were no longer viable, and she couldn't have a biological child without Seth's consent, which she lacked.She'd made the call to the storage lab to give her permission to destroy the eggs, making it contingent upon Seth's signing only because she was being petty and wanted him to take some responsibility. He'd so clearly blamed her for not having destroyed them when their marriage ended.

The thought brought a fresh wave of tears.

She caught the eye of another woman, several

feet away, who'd turned around while sunning herself. Annie caught the woman's instant recognition of someone in pain, saw the compassion on her face, and forced herself to head back up the sand toward her car. Though she wasn't openly crying, she felt like she was making a spectacle of herself. Walking around in a pool of grief.

To get her mind focused, to find some sense of reality in a world that had become nothing more than a blurred box lined with grief, she pulled out her phone. Remembering she had a text. Work. Something to distract her.

She couldn't give in to the pain. Couldn't let it take her down.

An only child, with both of her parents gone, she was it—the end of a remarkable love story. The last living element of her parents' unique and incredible bond. Unless she carried on the love that had created her.

What a shock it would be to everyone in her sphere were it to be known that the highly respected Lieutenant Annie Morgan had such a romantic side lurking inside her.

Back at her car, she faced the dark sedan, not ready to get in. And so she walked along the sidewalk edging the parking lot.

Forcing herself to move forward by touching the phone screen.

Opening her messages. Moving toward a big tree

offering shade so she could read the screen. Expecting an update on a case to pull her back to her real life. Needing it to do so.

I just sent a notarized statement preventing the destruction of the embryos until such a time as you make a second request to have it done. And then, upon your next contact with the facility, I release all ownership of the embryos. They are now yours to do with as you wish. —Seth

Annie dropped her phone.

Annie wanted to drive. For the ten minutes since she'd received Seth's text, she'd been trying to get herself together but had managed no more than picking up her phone, noting the newly cracked screen, and pacing the sidewalk.

Her mind reeled with all of the things she should be doing. Calls she had to make. She was shaking too much to worry with dialing. Or talking.

Seth had come through for her. She just couldn't believe it.

She needed to go to him. To walk into his arms and feel at home for the first time in ten years.

Which scared her more than anything.

She didn't fool herself, even for a second, that he'd changed his mind out of any latent desire to have children with her. Or with anyone.

He'd reversed his stance because he thought he owed her for not being able to support her career choice. She knew him well enough to understand that.

She couldn't make more of the reversal than it was. For all their sakes.

And she was going forward. There was not one single iota of doubt about that. Which meant that she had to wipe the idea of Seth Morgan being more than a biological element completely out of her picture.

As though just having the thought made life clear again, Annie's shaking slowed, and her strength and resolve returned. Fingering her screen carefully, she redialed the embryo storage facility, and then The Parent Portal, confirming her implantation on Saturday's schedule. And then, stopping only to visit a phone store to purchase the newer model she'd been needing anyway, she headed back to Marie Cove, determined that her life was going to be happier than she'd ever known before.

Determined to fight back against any memory of Seth, past or present, that tried to burst her newly formed bubble of joy. A feat made more difficult by the fact that her heart was not only filled with memories of her recent visit with him, but also with gratitude to him for having just made it possible for her dreams to come true.

She was firmly resolved, though. She spent the next couple of days taking care of business, mostly cases, overseeing her small group of detectives, advising, assigning committee work. On Friday, she entered the interrogation room to get a confession that saved a young woman from having to testify in an abuse case against her uncle. She went to dinner with and brought home budget paperwork.

Friday night was the hardest, anticipation for the next day's appointment filling her with such a myriad of emotions that she had to struggle to maintain her equilibrium. She'd been meaning to spend some time in the room in her home that she'd chosen for the nursery due to its close proximity to the master suite, but nixed that idea as images and conversations from her past immediately swamped her.

She left the room, but the memories wouldn't let go.

Recollections of the plans she and Seth had made in their San Diego home as they planned for the birth of their first child. Their painting the nursery together, laughing, crying and making love in the process. Their inability to conceive as planned, Seth being in law school, her re-upping in the navy, putting off her own education and career plans until he graduated, and then the fertility tests… It had all been such a volatile time.

It was no wonder she'd felt…somewhat relieved to get deployment orders.

When the familiar guilt for those feelings started to descend, Annie grabbed her keys and left the house. Thinking she'd head to the Irish pub that had become a gathering place for law enforcement. No beer for her that night—or the foreseeable future—but she could get an appetizer. Listen to the chatter...

Instead, she found herself driving to Mission Viejo, a larger city just north of Marie Cove. She'd never lived there, but had a dynasty of living relatives she'd never met. Her mother's family. They owned mansions. The Whitakers were in textiles, among other things. And probably politics, too, though they stayed squeaky clean. Annie had done her research over the years. Starting when they'd offered to pay for her education at an elite university upon her high school graduation. An offer she'd ignored.

And culminating more recently in her receipt of yet another request for contact from her mother's mother, whom she'd never met. Annie's grandmother had been making the requests via an attorney for many years, but that last request had included a five-page letter. Clara had bared her soul and admitted that she was writing without her husband's knowledge. Admitted that her life was empty, a charade of false smiles and empty platitudes without Chelsea and Annie.

She'd talked about obligations. Choices.

A single text message or attorney-delivered note would be enough to bring the woman comfort, Clara said. She'd respect all mandates for response guidelines. Clara would do whatever Annie needed, wanted, or requested, would abide by any stipulation Annie had, if they could please have contact.

Annie had grown up with a very clear understanding that the Whitakers were cut off because they'd done the same to her mother when her father was alive, and only tried to get back in touch after he was gone. They'd called her father worthless, a bum, bad news, and disowned their daughter when she married him so he wouldn't get their fortune. Not because Danny Bolin had ever given reason to think poorly of him; they'd just thought him beneath their daughter. So, Annie had read Clara's letter and calmly put it away.

But that Friday night, as she was shedding everything she'd left behind, the letter came back to her. She wasn't going to make contact, but she drove by the gated and maturely landscaped property where Clara Whitaker still lived with her husband of more than sixty years. The home where Chelsea had been raised. She'd like to have driven there with her mother, to hear stories of climbing that tree, or being locked out of that gate. To know how it felt to have been a child running through the acres of lush grass.

And when she was done sitting there, she drove home, took a hot shower and went to bed.

To attempt to sleep through the rest of the last night of her old life.

Chapter Four

He didn't know the time of Annie's appointment. She'd said Saturday, not indicating morning or afternoon, early or late. So, Seth waited from early morning on. Just needing to know that Annie had done the deed. He decided to forgo a game of golf with the general and others he usually played with so he could take the call in privacy when it came. She hadn't said she'd call. But he was certain she would. Annie was just that way—crossing all *t*'s, dotting all *i*'s. Surely, he was a *t* or an *i*.

He chose to spend the day in his office. One of his current cases—a young sailor named Hunter Bradley, accused of robbery with assault, having no alibi but an exemplary record—held his attention. The corpsman was sitting in jail, fearing that his entire future was imploding while he remained powerless to help himself, and Seth was going to do what he could to alleviate his stress.

From his initial look at the situation, including arrest statements, he wasn't completely convinced of the sailor's innocence, but he wasn't at all convinced of his guilt, either.

And maybe he was taking the case a bit too much to heart due to his current circumstances. The kid reminded him of Annie. From the time he'd first met her, she'd been passionate about helping young people in unfortunate circumstances get or keep their lives on track so they could lead productive, meaningful lives, contributing to society in a good way. Because of her father, he knew. Which was why she'd been so adamant about going into social work.

Who could ever have foreseen that, instead, because of some fluke assignment, she'd find her calling, her ability to help, in law enforcement?

Who could ever have foreseen that the day would pass, that The Parent Portal clinic hours would be over, without him hearing from her?

Seth called his department investigator before he left the office late that Saturday afternoon, telling him about the list he'd just sent over, things for the officer to look into pursuant to the Bradley case. He made it home, into his swimsuit and through twenty laps in the landscaped pool in his backyard before dialing his phone again.

Dripping wet, a towel around his neck, he stood out in the privacy of his walled-in backyard, looked at the orange trees, the bougainvillea, and waited for Annie to pick up. Had she had the procedure, and had just opted not to call? A guy couldn't get on with things, couldn't let go, until he knew whether or not she'd gotten implanted.

"Hello?" He could hear the firmness in her tone, the no-nonsense, capable and strong lieutenant talking, and she sounded like she'd developed a cold, too.

Or had been crying.

He knew his Annie. She'd been crying.

His gut sank and he stepped up to the diving board he rarely used, knowing that he wasn't free until the process she'd put in motion was done. Which he'd pretty much determined happened once she was inseminated. Then they were no longer dealing with joint embryos; it would be all on her. She'd be engaged in a new process—the growing and birthing of *her* child.

"Seth? You there?"

She'd recognized the incoming call. "Yes. Sorry. I…there was…a distraction just as you picked up." He stood there on the board, gazing out into the clear blue water. "I'm just calling to follow up," he told her. "Just making sure that you don't need anything else from me." There could be an errant signature. Some

form or another particular on which the storage lab,
or The Parent Portal, would require his sign-off. He
didn't want some unexpected, random call from any
of them in the coming days.

When he shut the door this time, it had to stay
shut.

"Nope, we're done."

That was it. Giving him no reassurance at all,
since he didn't know any details of what had been
done. The ownership papers? The implantation?

Did the embryos even exist anymore?

"What does that mean, exactly?"

"I don't need anything more from you." Her
voice might have wobbled on that last bit, like she
wasn't quite done crying. He could have imagined
the sound, but didn't think so.

He couldn't hang up without knowing that she was
okay. Not if he wanted to have any peace in his head.

"Did you make today's appointment?"

Or, God forbid, had they already destroyed the
eggs by the time she got back with the lab? He'd
made clear in the legal document he'd sent that they
weren't to do anything until they'd spoken with her
again. He should have texted her first, then sent the
document. He'd just wanted to let her know it was
done—and be done.

Her answer wasn't coming quickly enough.

Sweating now, he sat on the board, needing to
dive headfirst into the depths of the pool. But didn't

dare test the phone's water-resistant capabilities. If he lost her, she might not pick back up.

"Annie?" he prompted after several seconds.

"Y-yes. Yes, I'm here," she said. "And yes, I had the appointment."

She had. And hadn't called. And why would she? He was telling himself not to ask when he said, "Did everything go okay?"

"Yes."

"So…you're implanted?" Breath held, he awaited the reply.

"Yes."

The whoosh that burst through him was far more than air in his lungs. The force of it leaving him a bit dizzy, he tried to find reason within himself. To ground himself. While suspended on the end of a board with enough give to rock up and down with his movement.

Annie had their embryos inside her uterus.

He couldn't grasp the reality of it.

"I have to go, Seth."

He couldn't say goodbye. Left it up to her to do so. Waited. And eventually said, "Are you sorry you did it? Having regrets?"

That could be an issue he'd need to know about. If his biological child was unwanted…

"Absolutely not."

"Then why have you been crying?" There, he put

the fact on the table. He knew her. Couldn't pretend otherwise.

"Because I'm hormonal," she told him, but still didn't hang up.

Because she was hanging on? To him? No, that didn't follow. He was the one who'd called.

She'd had the procedure. No more guessing. It was over. A done deal.

"You were never one to get overly emotional," he found the sense to say. "Not even when you were taking hormones." Part of their early fertility efforts. Before the more complete testing of both of them that had ultimately determined that there was no scientific reason for them not to conceive.

She said nothing. And didn't hang up.

"Tell me why you were crying."

"You don't want to know."

"I wouldn't be asking if I didn't want to know." The setting sun left a soft glow over the yard. The water. Seth relaxed into it as he stayed on the phone with Annie.

"How can you be so sure I was crying?"

"I know you."

"Well, I know you, too, and trust me to know that you don't want to know why I was crying."

It was like they were at the beginning again—her a young recruit in Sealift Command and him a more seasoned sailor with US Fleet Forces, but no more mature when it came to the love that hit them both so powerfully. And quickly.

"I want to know anyway." Nothing kid-like about that fact. He lifted his thigh, feeling the sting of board peeling from stuck skin, but didn't get up. Just lifted the other leg to free it, as well.

"I was crying for you, Seth."

For him? Because she wanted him, was crying out for him, in need of him? Heart pounding, he acknowledged that she'd been right. He didn't want to know.

There was nothing good to come of him knowing that.

"I'm finally seeing my dream come to reality. Today, I got the single most thing I've wanted since I can remember…to have a baby inside me. But you…"

She let the words trail off, and he was done, too. "You have no reason to pity me, Annie," he told her quite clearly. "I didn't have any idea of the breadth of opportunities the world had to offer back then. I've reached the culmination of dreams that I hadn't even known were possible." As he sat there, he couldn't envision anything clearly, but he'd been to so many fantastic places all over the world, had been wined and dined like a king, by kings—or rulers of nations at least. He was more of a somebody than he'd ever imagined being, having done work that mattered on a national level to his country and would continue to matter long after he was gone.

"Then I'm happy for you, Seth," Annie said, her tone growing stronger. "Happy for both of us. We're both finally getting what we wanted."

He could do nothing but agree with that. And when she told him goodbye, say goodbye back. It was done.

Over.

Leaving his phone on the edge of the board, Seth fell forward into the water and sank to the bottom.

Stayed there until the lack of air in his lungs required action.

And then slowly surfaced.

Annie lay low on Sunday. Dr. Miller had told her she was fine to resume normal activity after the time she spent resting at the clinic immediately following the procedure. But she opted to give the two embryos the best opportunity to adhere calmly and strongly inside her uterus.

Calmly and strongly. Her mother used to say the words a lot in trying times. They'd been her father's mantra.

She read some. A lighthearted tale of sisters trying to make their way in a small town, but put the book down when one character suddenly introduced a love interest. Watched some TV, but not for long. Every show seemed to have some kind of romantic element or another. With her tablet poised on her rib cage, she perused baby furniture for a while. Just testing herself to see what stood out to her, so she'd know for the future.

There'd be no actual baby shopping until a pregnancy was confirmed.

And she avoided all phone calls. Her team knew to 911-text her if something came up—which was the protocol for all of them on their days off. Anyone else, even Christa McGinnis, a single cop like herself who was the closest thing she had to a best friend, would leave a message.

She didn't want to talk to Christa. The woman was a great cop. She'd know something was different. And Annie wasn't telling anyone about her baby plans until she had something to tell. No way she was going to have people looking at her with a question in their eyes, wanting to know if she'd heard anything. Or pity her if she got her period.

She lived alone. That meant tackling life's most intimate issues alone.

When she knew she had a baby coming…then she'd open the door. And Christa would be the first one inside. She planned to ask her colleague to be the baby's guardian in the event that anything happened to her…

Because Seth most definitely wouldn't want to raise his child.

She was getting ahead of herself.

And the child wasn't *his*. Half of each embryo had been, but he'd signed away ownership of them. Per

Parent Portal policy, and legal documents he'd signed years ago, she could contact him if there was ever any need to do so—and he could contact her, too, if ever he wanted to ask how the child was doing, or request contact.

She didn't have to give him contact, though. She did have to let him know how the child was doing, if he asked. He wouldn't.

Propped up on pillows, she lay there on her couch, in leggings and a long, button-down shirt, and stared at the ceiling. Saw a smudge and thought about having the ceilings painted. Beige instead of their current white. Beige would be warmer for any little being who might be spending months lying on his or her back, staring up at that ceiling.

She needed to clean the fans, too.

Stuff that should happen whether she ever had a child in her home or not.

Her toes were cold. Reaching for the gray-and-white chenille throw on the back of her couch—not really her preferred color, but it had been a gift from a desk clerk—she threw it over her feet. And for a second there, saw Seth's hand smoothing it down over her feet, tucking it in.

He wasn't there. But the memory was so strong she felt his presence. She'd always had cold feet. And he'd always covered them for her. Even after several years of marriage, he'd still been conscientious enough, aware of her enough, caring enough, to do that.

Tears sprang up again, as they'd been doing since the procedure the day before. Since she'd seen him again, really. And realized that she didn't want anyone but him to be the father of her child.

When he'd told her no, it was as though her entire plan faded to nothing. Because she couldn't have any current eggs fertilized, she'd told herself. But the truth was, she wanted Seth's child. Made no sense, was completely illogical, but there it was.

She didn't want him. Couldn't ever trust him with her heart again. That truth was unequivocal, and she didn't question it. Or fight it.

But…if they could possibly, maybe in a year or two in the future when the baby was able to walk and talk, interact more, Seth could play a bit of a part…

The thought stopped the tears, so she let it exist. Tried to focus on other things. Clicked the TV back on. Scrolled through channels. Turned it off. Chose to go with music instead. Made herself a kale-and-cabbage salad with sunflower seeds and honey mustard dressing. Grabbed some crackers for good measure and settled in a chair at the small table in the eating alcove in her kitchen.

She didn't eat at home enough.

Her dining room was generally only used when she had people over.

And two of three bedrooms hadn't been slept in…

ever. She'd bought the house new. She could vouch for those sleeping-less rooms.

One would be a nursery.

Hopefully.

She hadn't taken a bite of her salad yet. It was dinnertime and she just wasn't hungry. But like she had for breakfast and lunch, she picked up the silverware and did what she had to do. Put food in her mouth, chewed and swallowed. Gave energy to the little embryos inside her, hoping and praying that at least one of them chose to hang on to her.

Chances weren't really in her favor. Not on a first try. And at thirty-eight years of age. A major reason why she wasn't telling anyone about her efforts yet.

She finished every bite of the salad. Rinsed the plate and put it in the dishwasher. Wiped the cupboards of her cheery, bright kitchen with its abundance of windows, and went back to the living room couch. Keeping her uterus mostly supine might not help. But it couldn't hurt. She had the day to give it. Had to do everything she could do to bring her child to life.

But was afraid to think about there actually being a baby. She had eight to twelve days to get through before she'd know. Couldn't spend them dreaming of a reality that might not exist. She was strong, but even she had her limits.

And the damned television didn't seem to be able to produce anything other than people having, finding or wanting partners. Why hadn't she ever noticed that before?

She didn't have, wasn't looking, didn't want.

Seth's face came to her mind's eye again. Not the younger version from the past, but the man she'd seen just four days before. The one with some wrinkles at the edges of those deep blue eyes. And a hint of silver at the edges of his thick blond hair. And heat flooded her privates. Energy pooled there in a way it hadn't in far too many years.

Click, click, click. Annie landed on a horror flick. Something she'd never in a million years choose. She got horror enough in everyday life. But what did she know? Maybe she'd like it...

Less than a minute in she was scrolling again. And when her phone rang, grabbed it up, relieved to have someone to talk to. Even if it was a robocall. There'd be a voice other than her own at her ear...

Her world settled for an instant when she saw the name on the screen.

Chapter Five

Seth. Almost as though...

"Hello?" She had to pick up. They'd created those embryos together, whether he still had legal right to them or not.

"I hope this isn't a bad time."

"No." She wanted to sit up. To pace or go outside and sit at the little play pool that had come with the new house—in a yard much too big for it. But she remained exactly as she was, leaning back against pillows from both spare beds. "What's up?"

"I'm sorry to butt in on you, but I had some questions that I needed to clear up..."

Of course, he did. Always the lawyer. And always

studying every aspect of any event in his life. Ticking off a to-do list.

Seth's ways used to drive her mother nuts. Chelsea had been far more of a free spirit than her daughter or son-in-law. Meanwhile, Seth's attention to detail was one of the things that had endeared him to Annie.

She'd figured his sticking to his lists was a guarantee that he'd always be there for her. Because it was on the list—their list of wedding vows, written by them, for them.

"I've...uh...done some reading..."

No surprise there, either, but... "About what?"

"Implantation."

Okay. She wasn't going to read more into that than was there. Seth was... Seth.

But...she was glad he hadn't been able to just sign his name and walk away. The Seth she'd thought she'd married wouldn't have been able to. It was nice to know she hadn't completely misjudged him.

"Things have changed a lot in the last decade," she told him.

"The success rate...it's not..."

"I know," she interrupted, her tone soft and completely reassuring. She might have a thought or two about him someday knowing his child, but no way did she want him thinking he was going to start looking out for her again—not in any capacity.

"So...you're prepared... Do you plan to try again if it doesn't take?"

He was no longer part owner of the material. But the agreement they'd signed at The Parent Portal, and that she'd adhered to when she'd been implanted, gave him the right to ask.

"I do." She had an ample supply of money saved. She made a good salary, wasn't an extravagant person, and had no one else to spend it on.

Or…more honestly…she'd been saving for a college fund she'd hoped she'd need some day. For her offspring.

"I'm only using two embryos at a time," she told him. They'd gone through the process twice, just to be safe. Had retrieved twenty-nine of her healthy eggs. Fourteen had become embryos. She had seven tries to get it right.

Did he remember the details to do the math? She couldn't let it matter one way or another.

"Was that it? One question?" she asked when the line hung silent. It was awkward, the two of them knowing each other so well, but not having really talked, except by the occasional text and email, for almost a decade.

"No," he said. "I have another. Assuming one of your implantations is successful, and there are embryos left, what is your plan for them?"

"I don't have a plan for them." If she had any left, she'd…keep them.

"You have a plan, even if you don't know it," he said then. "Would you destroy them?"

"No."

"Then you plan to keep them."

She smiled. Remembering, suddenly, a much younger Seth. They'd been dating only a few weeks and she'd told him she couldn't go out with him on a Friday night. She'd been living on base and had had to have an exterminator in, hadn't wanted him to suggest that he wait with her. He'd asked pointed questions that really had nothing to do with what he wanted to know—when what he'd really wanted to determine was whether or not she was going out with someone else.

"I plan to keep them," she said, not really sure what he was after, but knowing, instinctively, that her keeping the embryos wasn't it.

"You plan to have more than one child, then? Assuming things would work out allowing that to happen?"

They'd always said they wanted kids in even numbers. Four preferably, but at least two. Because they'd both been only children themselves.

"I'm not thinking that way right now," she told him. He'd changed, and so had she. "I'm not saying I won't do that, just that I'm thirty-eight, Seth. Everything I have, every bit of energy and hope, is going into bringing a healthy child into my world. One will be a miracle."

When they'd been thinking in twos, there'd been two of them.

"Okay, then…well, if it turns out you need my signature on anything there at the clinic, don't worry about asking for it. You'll get it, no questions asked."

And there they were…at his reason for calling. She could let him off the hook. But didn't.

"I'm sorry, Annie. I got all up into myself and had no right to be angry with you the other day."

The words felt good to hear. She let them replay, relaxed into them. And then said, "Apology accepted."

"Will you…uh…let me know the results…one way or another?"

"If you want me to," she told him, and then, for both of them added the all-important reminder, "It's your right, per The Parent Portal agreement we both signed."

"I want you to," he said.

And though she tried to hold on to it, her heart soared a little higher.

On Monday, Seth was called in to consult on a past project, a legal issue, that had been resolved several years before. The case involved a bi-country team of military personnel working together to further each other's interests and the logistics of how that would work. He'd been on the legal team that had handled the situation and had been the one who ultimately put forth the plan to which both sides had agreed; now the referendum needed some tweaking.

He was fine with the work, just didn't like that it required him to be out of the country for three days that next week.

He had no good reason to not want to be gone right now. Though he'd tied up the Hunter Bradley situation, he still wasn't positive the young sailor was innocent, but because his guilt wasn't provable, either, Seth had managed to get the charges dropped. And prayed the kid would make the most of his second chance.

Leaving the country was usually a perk of the job to him. And he could just as easily receive a call from Annie overseas as he could at home in San Diego. Technology was a wonderful thing.

If either of the embryos lived, she wouldn't know for more than a week. And it wasn't like he had any action items on that matter, either way.

But as he lay in bed each night that he was away, he remembered one evening when he'd awoken late to find that she'd had her period. Why that night kept coming back to him, he didn't know. But it had the day she'd first visited him the week before and continued to stay with him.

She'd been so heartbroken. Worse than he'd ever seen her.

He'd been afraid that night.

Afraid for her. Afraid of losing her to something neither of them could control.

And then he'd ended up losing her anyway because he'd been unable to control his own aversion to who she needed to be.

That lack in himself…yes, well, it was why he'd determined, after a second try, a second failed marriage, to focus on what he did well instead of thinking he needed something he wasn't made for. He might have thought he wanted a wife. To have a family. But ultimately, he must not have wanted it badly enough.

After all, he'd been the one who'd walked out of both marriages.

Walked out on who Annie had become. And his second wife—he hadn't been able to make her happy, either.

Lying in the dark the third night, his hands behind his head, staring at shadows, he couldn't hide from himself. He was afraid again. Afraid that Annie would have her period while he was gone and there'd be no way he could get to her.

If it happened, it would devastate her. She might not believe that. But he knew it.

And knew he had to get back to San Diego, just in case.

The next day, working furiously, he finished his work, and then, on his own dime rather than waiting for military transport, he got a flight that same night. Knew marked relief when he touched down in the United States. And again, when he landed at San Diego's one-runway airport.

He was surprised to see an email from Captain Ben Kinder of the San Diego Police Department when he got to his desk the next day. The message was about the youth task force Annie was heading. He hadn't expected her to actually follow through in connecting him with any team she was on—even peripherally. He answered immediately, agreeing to meet with Kinder to see how the program could help teenagers he met through the community center.

Seth felt a lift in his mood, too. Knowing that Annie had paved a way for the two of them to be joined—even if from afar. In more than one way.

And yet, that connection seemed to make the waiting that much more acute. Was she pregnant? Or wasn't she?

During the day, work and volunteering helped.

And at night, after dinner out or beers with buddies, he waited.

She'd said she'd let him know either way.

As each day passed, he got more geared up. She'd said either way, and if he wasn't hearing from her, one could assume that meant she hadn't started her period. There'd been a time when he'd kept up to date on her cycle, back when they'd been fully focused on their goal of starting a family.

Who'd have thought a decade later, he'd be right back there, homing in on her cycle, but not to have a child of his own? The thought occurred to him Monday morning as he stood in line at his favorite ocean-view coffee shop not far from the base, a week and two days after the implantation. Plans had changed. But there was a plan. As long as there was a plan, things were good. He ordered his coffee black—nothing frothy, creamy or sweet—slid his bank card into the chip slot and went out to walk for a minute before heading back to his car and onto base.

A couple of women he passed on the way out the door glanced at him and smiled. Tourists, he figured. He'd learned long ago that it was the uniform that attracted the attention far more than the man inside it.

Still, proud of the rows of bars he'd earned, he puffed out his chest a bit as he held the door open for an older couple coming inside. He'd become a man he felt good about. Had made the right choices for the person he was.

He wasn't quite grinning as he walked away, and almost dropped his coffee as he heard the soft tones of a partial stanza from an old jazz song play from the phone attached to his belt. He'd specifically set the ringtone to be unassuming in the presence of others, but to alert him to an immediate need to answer his phone.

"Annie?" he asked, juggling hot coffee and his cell phone at the same time. Instead of heading down the sidewalk and around to take the long way to his car, he headed across the street to a sidewalk that kept the ocean in sight.

"I'm fulfilling my obligation to let you know that

I received the results of a pregnancy test a few minutes ago," she said.

And he knew. The words were professional but the wavering tone of her voice…

"You're pregnant," he said.

"Yes." Her tone changed a bit, grew stronger, and he wondered if his was the first call she'd made. Was he getting the news almost as soon as she was?

Why that should matter, he couldn't say, but he couldn't deny the surge of emotion that quickened his pace for a step or two.

"However, there is still a greater than normal risk of miscarriage," she warned. Warning herself as well as him? He heard the hint of fear in her voice.

How in the hell could you know so much about someone, remember so much, a decade apart?

"You knew that going in," he reminded, not to make light of the situation, but to guide her focus back to a less volatile place. "You're right where you wanted to be." It did no good to focus on the bad that could happen. That simply made potential negativity a bigger part of your current reality when, in fact, unless it came to be, it wasn't real.

"I know. And…thank you for reminding me of that fact."

He nodded as he walked. "So, what now?"

"Just monitoring things. Taking vitamins. Minimizing risks. And otherwise, life as usual."

"And your hormone levels? Are they high

enough?" If not, she'd be taking hormones. He remembered the drill. And he had refreshed himself on it over the past ten days, too.

"Yes."

There was no more to say. He had no intention of lengthening any conversations that could lead them into getting to know each other better. Sharing things drew people closer together. He and Annie didn't need that.

So... "Congratulations on the great news, Annie. I'm truly happy for you." Surprisingly, he was. In all of the days of waiting, he hadn't been able to get a good read on himself. Of course, for Annie, he'd wanted her first attempt to be a success, but hadn't been able to determine where he stood personally with it all.

Now he saw his lack of attachment as a good thing. Saw it as exactly what they needed. What was right and healthy for both of them.

"Thank you," she said. "I need to go. I have a lot of calls to make."

"You just found out?" He'd wondered but didn't *need* to know. But the moment was kind of...set apart.

Scientifically a miracle was taking place. Biology that had taken place a decade ago was producing a human being.

"I'm still sitting in my car outside The Parent Portal."

The admission hit him in the gut. She'd come

straight to him first, with the news. He wanted the information. Had no good place to store it.

Which left him in a quandary.

"You better get calling, then. I'm sure there are a lot of people waiting to hear." People he'd never met. Didn't even know about.

"No, actually, no one else knows yet," she said. "Until I had your permission to use the embryos, I didn't even know I'd be going through the process, and with the possibility of it taking so long, I didn't want to endure added emotional situations with people checking in, or giving sympathy…"

His Annie had been like that. Always looking out for others' emotional health, sometimes to the risk of her own, in his opinion. And yet, he'd loved that characteristic. Annie was one of the least selfish people he'd ever met. Had that maybe made it easier for him to be *more* selfish? Had he gotten away with too much?

He wished he knew. Looking back, it didn't look that way to him, but folks rarely saw themselves in true light…

And even as his thoughts sped by, he saw what he was doing. Making it about him.

"I hate that you're going through it all alone," he told her. Acknowledging the instant pull he'd felt when she'd said the words. Admitting the feelings were there. Him not wanting her there all alone. Him wanting to be there for her.

"I won't be," she assured him. "I'd decided to wait until I had a positive pregnancy, and then to start letting people in…"

Good. He was off the hook. There'd be relief in that. Hopefully soon.

"So…you'll keep me informed?" he asked.

"I'll absolutely let you know if anything happens." She came back with a surety she had every right to. "If the pregnancy doesn't last… And, of course, I'll notify you when the baby is born, if that's information you want."

He'd been put in his place. A good thing for both of them. All three of them, his mind amended quickly. "Take care of you, Annie," he said, wishing her well from his heart as he ended the call.

He headed back to his car immediately upon re-holstering his phone. Drove to work, onto base and parked in his reserved place. He went back to living his life.

But knew, even as he denied the facts, that everything had just changed.

Annie was pregnant from the embryos they'd made together.

Whether he was included in any part of the pregnancy or the child's life, whether he never had a single legal right, he was going to be a father.

Chapter Six

Annie's Monday passed in a blur of activity and a roller coaster of emotion. She was fully present and focused on her job, but a tinge of surrealness was overshadowing everything she did. She told the captain, her immediate superior, about her positive pregnancy test. Talked to him about being on limited duty—meaning that she wouldn't be out on the streets, which wasn't in her job description anyway—and let him know that she was planning to take about six weeks' maternity leave. She not only loved her job—she needed it. If all went well, she was going to have a family to support.

And she went to dinner with Christa, who'd followed her down to Marie Cove PD from LA when Annie had taken the lieutenant job. Christa's husband, the love of her life, also a cop, had been killed on the job a couple of years before Annie's move and Christa had been ready for the change.

Christa knew how badly Annie wanted to be a mother. It was an area where they differed: Christa, who loved kids, didn't want to bring any into the world. Just like Christa didn't want to be a lieutenant. She wanted to be in the streets, solving crimes. Protecting other people's kids and loved ones.

Her friend was fully supportive, excited, even, when Annie delivered her news over the Asian chicken salads they'd both ordered. Right up until she told her that she'd been inseminated with embryos created with her ex-husband.

"You used...you're carrying Seth's baby?"

Quickly shaking her head, even while the words reverberated through her, she said, "No. I'm having my baby. He wants nothing to do with it. And legally signed away ownership."

Frowning, her dark curls framing her porcelain doll features, Christa leaned across the table and said, "He did that years ago? When you divorced?"

Smoothing her blouse over the brown pants she'd chosen that morning, Annie shook her head. "He did two weeks ago Wednesday." She looked her friend in the eye, needing Christa to see what she couldn't see herself. "I went to see him."

Christa's fork froze in midair. Her jaw froze mid-chew. But her gaze worked overtime as she studied Annie.

"Are you okay?" was all she said when the perusal was done.

"Yeah." Annie nodded. Smiled even. "How can I not be? I just found out I'm going to be a mother!"

Christa's smile wasn't as big as it had been the first time Annie imparted the news. "Are you seeing him again?"

Shaking her head, Annie ran a hand through her hair, feeling the short strands slide like soft silk through her fingers. A familiar sensation. Familiar touch. "He wants to be notified when the baby's born."

"So…how was it, seeing him again?"

She touched her hair again. Needing to find a way to connect to who she knew herself to be. "Honestly, I don't know." Honestly, she didn't want to think about it. But needed Christa to have her back.

Which meant her friend needed to know what to watch out for.

"You know how much I loved him." Christa had never met Seth, but she'd seen the state Annie had been in when she'd heard that Seth had remarried. And had been present for coffee on too many mornings after.

"That's what worries me." Christa was no fool.

And didn't pull punches, either. "This situation is ripe for your heart to get broken all over again."

In some ways Christa knew her better than anyone else. They'd been through a lot together. Worked cases that left them with visuals neither of them would ever forget. Annie had been on duty with Christa when the call had come in that her husband had been shot. And Christa had been the one to stand beside Annie at her mother's funeral.

"When I saw him, the way our marriage ended was right there in the room, like a physical thing between us. I really think it's going to be okay."

"You do?" Christa's look was more nurturing than anything else.

"I do," Annie said, looking her friend straight in the eye. There was no way she'd be able to let something start up between her and Seth again. That kind of trust no longer existed for the two of them.

Which was why, if Seth did want a place in the baby's life at some point, she'd welcome his involvement. They weren't kids anymore. They'd both matured and had reached success in their lives without each other.

Not that she needed to get ahead of herself. Or start counting on a future with Seth in it—for her baby's sake. She was having a child alone. And with the newfound knowledge of that life growing inside her, she was happier than she'd ever been.

She felt the same a couple of hours later as she sat

in her living room, having just shut off the television, but not yet ready to go bed. She just wasn't sleepy. Her hand softly rubbing her belly in the lightweight flannel pants she'd pulled on with a short tank top, she quit fighting her mind. It jumped from thought to thought, vision to vision, memory to memory. Dr. Miller that morning, telling her that her test had come back positive. They'd had her in an examining room to deliver the news so she could have a consultation, either way. She kept thinking about the smile that lit up the doctor's eyes.

The grin on the clinic owner's face, and that of the receptionist as she'd made her way out of the clinic. Those people weren't regulars in her life, but they felt like family to her.

And her mom, who Annie knew was surely smiling with her from the spirit world.

And Seth? He'd seemed pleased. For her, of course, but still...

What was he doing on the eve of finding out that their embryo was coming to life? Probably working. Or out having a working dinner. Or a beer with someone.

A buddy.

Or a woman.

He could be on a date. For all she knew he was serious with someone. Maybe even living with her.

Would that woman know about the embryo? Had

he told her that his ex-wife was pregnant with their child?

Why hadn't Annie thought of that possibility before now?

And why did it matter either way?

Stop.

She repeated that to herself several times and resolved to redirect her thoughts, but they found their back to Seth. So much so that it was a relief when her phone rang.

Even if it meant a new case for her detectives, and a need to go into work.

Grabbing her cell off the end table, she saw the name on the screen, and when she answered, pretended that she was still as calm as if the caller had been someone from work.

"Seth? What's up?"

What's up? What's up? Like they were pals who spoke now and then? Or it was normal for him to be calling her at bedtime?

"I've got a concern," he told her. "I'm sorry to be calling so late, but I'm just leaving a dinner."

"No, it's fine," she told him, sitting up, leaning over with her arms on her knees, staring at shadows on the area rug that covered a big patch of the porcelain-tiled floor painted to resemble hardwood. "I'm still up. What's your concern?"

"I'd like to talk to you about having a legal guardianship set up in the event that something should happen to render you incapable of caring for the child."

That conversation wasn't any of his business. Not even through The Parent Portal agreement.

She opened her mouth to tell him so and closed it again. When they'd signed their contracts and made their embryos, they'd had every plan to raise any resultant children together. He'd done a good thing for her, honoring her request to have full ownership of those embryos.

And the one thought that was superseding all others... Seth was once again taking action to tend to the good care of the life resulting from their long-ago union.

Blinking back tears, she sat back, stared at the black television screen. "I plan to ask my friend Christa," she said.

Silence initially met her statement. She wasn't sure what to say to break it. Couldn't see enough to understand his current mindset, or determine how to proceed to a mutual understanding. Truth be told, she couldn't see enough into herself to know for sure what she wanted that mutual understanding to be.

She knew what it should be. What it had to be.

But the fact that he'd called...

What if, sometime in the future, they could actually be friends? What if he wanted a weekend visit with his baby? The child would benefit from knowing him. She had no doubt about that.

"When did you plan to ask her?"

He hadn't asked who Christa was. What she did for a living. How long Annie had known her. How well she knew her. All questions Annie would expect.

He probably wasn't asking because he knew he had no right to do so.

"Soon," she told him. "Before the baby's born, certainly." She wanted to tell him she'd told Christa about the baby over dinner. Wanted to tell him how excited her friend had been. But was also reminded of Christa's earlier worry, and her own knowledge that Seth could never again be a partner to her. Or even a close friend.

Those kinds of relationships took a trust that was impossible between them. How could you emotionally trust someone who'd left once your own needs posed emotional difficulties?

She got it. Even at the time, she'd understood his perspective. He'd lost his mother to law enforcement. Had been there when the official came to the door. He'd been understandably scarred.

But it had still ripped her heart out that her Seth hadn't had her back. Because while her head understood, her heart had needed him more than ever.

"I'm happy to do the legal paperwork for you, if you'd like. Actually," he continued, cutting off the polite refusal ready to roll off her tongue, "I'd prefer to do it. Or at least to have a chance to vet it."

What was he doing? "Seth…"

"I know… I have no rights. And I feel good about that. I'm not trying to insinuate myself onto you or the baby," he told her. "But this is all brand-new to me—the reality hasn't really even sunk in. I gave you the embryos because it was the right thing to do. Because I owe you more than I'll ever be able to give for letting you down in the past. And because it was your only chance to have what I know to be something you need more than pretty much anything else…"

That was true now. Once upon time, when he'd been her prince, he'd been what she'd needed more than anything else.

"You did me a solid, Seth. I'll be grateful forever."

"I'm not looking for gratitude. I'm trying to live with the results of having made a monumental decision very quickly. I don't regret doing what I did, and at the same time, I'm figuring out how I live responsibly, knowing that a young human being that is created from my biology is out in the world. I have a hundred percent faith in you, Annie. I have no concerns about the child's welfare with you there. But what if you're not around? That thought is on my mind."

A permanently closed part of her heart felt a shard of light suddenly shining. Painfully. He knew firsthand how a kid felt when he lost his mother. And Annie was in the same profession that had taken Seth's mother from him.

She'd known when she'd gone to him what she was asking of him. How could she not? His resistance to the risk of her career had been what had driven them apart.

Had she really thought when he'd given his permission that he'd made peace with the past? Or had she just not let herself go there?

The past was past. She'd laid those hurts to rest as well as anyone ever could. She was moving on to a new life now.

But how was Seth going to feel when he found out that Christa was a cop, too?

There was nothing he could do about any of it. He had no legal grounds to interfere with her life, or her plans.

There was no reason for her to worry herself about it all.

But… "I'd be happy to have you oversee the paperwork," she told him.

And then, holding back tears, told him good-night.

Seth drove up to LA to have dinner with his father the following Sunday, six days after he'd last spoken with Annie. He and his dad generally met about twice a month, and with his recent trip, they'd missed a week. He drove by the Marie Cove exit without stopping. As tempting as it might be to see where Annie was living, to reassure himself that she and her child were well positioned, or maybe, more truthfully, out of sheer curiosity—he did not get off the freeway.

For the most part he was doing okay. Working ungodly hours. And volunteering when he wasn't working. Maybe hanging out at the officers' club a bit more than normal, having two beers instead of the one he usually had, and spending more time in the gym on base, but life was moving on and he was keeping up with it. Well…

So yeah, he thought of Annie a lot. Anytime he had a break at work. When he met with a single mother at the community center. Sitting on a stool at the club. Running on the treadmill. And when a fellow officer he'd seen a time or two asked him to a yacht dinner function and he turned her down.

She'd seemed to be getting somewhat attached and he'd sworn off allowing that after his second divorce. He wasn't leaving any more women in tears.

Randy Morgan was late getting home, and Seth had a pork roast in the oven when his father walked in the door of the home in which Seth had grown up. Randy, at sixty-one, still stood an inch taller than Seth's six feet , and his hair was all gray now, but still as thick as it had ever been. The man worked out every day on the equipment that had been in their basement gym—in updated versions—since before Seth was born.

Seth had no intention of telling his father about Annie's visit, her request, or the result of such, and had warned himself to make certain that he didn't give his father any inkling of the things on his mind. Randy, who still worked full-time as a county deputy, was not only observant, but when he decided to get to the bottom of something, was like a pit bull.

His father spent the whole evening talking about the case that he'd just come from working. An arrest he'd been called to make on a man living outside of city limits—someone who was wanted in a couple of cold-case murders, found through genealogical DNA.

"We get there, and the guy just starts shooting." Randy shook his head, gaze lowered, as though he was trying not to see what was in his mind's eye. They were sitting at the table, the food was there, but his father hadn't served up his plate yet.

Seth listened intently. Always hearing the legal implications, wanting to make sure that nothing was going to come back on his father—one of the best cops he'd ever known. And hearing his father's inner need to protect the innocent. It was always there. In everything Randy did.

And in everything Annie did, too. He got the implication. Annie hadn't just made a choice to go into law enforcement because she'd found that she liked the work. Or even because she'd found she was good at it.

She'd made the choice because she'd been driven to do so.

He knew that now.

And had known it back then, too. Which was why, when he'd realized his fears weren't going to change, he'd told her he'd thought they should separate. He'd met someone else during the months she'd been deployed—another JAG attorney. And while there was no way he'd ever have been unfaithful to his wife, the fact that he'd been drawn to the other woman had scared the hell out of him. If he and Annie had been as close and connected as he'd thought, he wouldn't have wanted to confide in, or want to have dinner with another woman.

Randy was shaking his head. "The woman...she couldn't have been more than twenty-five, and those kids...he was going to kill them all..."

Randy and the deputies with him had managed to shoot the man first, saving the young woman and her kids who, it turned out, were the man's daughter and grandchildren. One of the crimes the man was wanted for was killing his wife—the young woman's mother. And, as it happened, the daughter was wanted for murder, too. Of her husband, the father of her children.

It was a twisted tale. One of the worst Randy had ever seen. And there was more. They'd found the guy's DNA through a brother who'd been incarcerated for decades for killing their drunken father— a man who'd probably beat on them but who, at the time of the murder, had been asleep in his bed.

Randy eventually filled his plate. And while they

ate, they talked about the charges being brought, arraignment, bail possibilities based on the charges... all things that Seth could contribute to in a way that reassured his father that justice would be done.

"It's like it was in their blood," Randy said as the two of them stood in the driveway by Seth's car as Seth was getting ready to leave just after dark. The dishes were done. They had played a game or two of pool on the table that had also been in the basement, along with laundry facilities, for Seth's entire life.

"This whole DNA thing, it's important," Randy continued. Seth's father had always been a talker. Seth had figured maybe that was why he'd tended to be more the reticent type. He'd had little opportunity to get a word in edgewise when he was growing up. "I keep thinking about all those deaths..."

Seth didn't disagree with his father. He'd learned enough, seen enough real cases, to know that certain propensities came from certain chemicals in the brain, or an odd wiring of other biological components.

With his father's emotional upheaval so clearly in the forefront of his mind, Seth headed back down toward San Diego with a mind more active than peaceful. DNA mattered. Biology mattered. His genetics—a compilation of his father's family and his mother's—were unique, providing distinct chemical characteristics and genetic combinations that could determine some of a child's struggles and challenges, as well as successes. How could that impact the child Annie was carrying?

The thought, once there, wouldn't let go, and he got his father on the phone. Asked him to gather up the genealogy paperwork his grandmother had compiled years ago, before her death, and to add to it whatever his father knew, and then send it to him. He told his father that he was doing a personal assessment, which he most definitely was, and left it at that. And Randy, being one of the greatest dads ever, sent it back before Seth had completed even the three-hour drive home. His dad didn't know a lot in terms of family diagnoses, but said he'd written what he knew as a cover page and he'd added the few things he knew about Seth's mom's family.

The task had been good for Randy. Seth could tell from the calmer tone in his father's voice. He'd had a particularly rough day on the job, and Seth had been able to ease a bit of residual emotional overload for him.

It felt good—being in a relationship where he contributed positively. And it felt good having a father.

Something his child would never know.

Chapter Seven

The text came through Wednesday night, right before bedtime.

Are you up?

Waiting for a cup of herbal tea to heat in the microwave, Annie read the text on her watch. She'd earlier marked a big yellow *X* on the calendar hanging on her fridge. Eighteen days since implantation. She'd made it through a full second week of pregnancy, as all of the previous colorful marks proclaimed. She was using primary colors, and the bold reds, yellows and blues were making a rainbow of celebration each day that passed.

Work remained largely the same, as she'd opted to wait to tell anyone besides Christa and the captain about her pregnancy until she'd passed the third critical month. For the same reasons she'd chosen not to tell anyone about the implantation. She had enough keeping her mind distracted with worry without people constantly asking her how she was doing, showing concern, or even just giving her looks of curiosity. And in case something went wrong, she'd be much better equipped to deal with the residual grief if she could just go to work and not have everyone know.

And it wasn't like her job required her to be out on the streets, or in positions of danger, on a regular basis anymore. Her only real time with perpetrators was in interrogation rooms, and even that was only as needed, when a detective requested her expertise.

Her phone was across the room, on the counter by the archway leading into the great room. That area flowed into a large living space, where her couch beckoned for a few minutes of streaming a mindless sitcom to clear her mind before bed.

She was in wind-down mode. Didn't need to deal with anything further that day.

Most particularly not the ex-husband who seemed to be creeping back into her daily consciousness at a rate that she knew to be somewhat concerning. Noteworthy, at the very least.

Whatever Seth needed to tell her, or ask, could

wait for morning. It wasn't like the baby's life could be in danger. She was the one in possession of any current embryonic development information that existed. And right now, that information consisted of the news that she was still pregnant and exhibiting no signs of anything out of the ordinary.

Everything was status quo. Thank God.

And maybe Seth needed to know that. He cared, at least a little bit. Even if she hadn't known him so well, she'd have figured out his phone calls showed a level of thought toward her situation. Most particularly the request to see paperwork regarding the baby's guardianship.

Maybe that was why he'd texted. Just to follow up on legalities. She'd said she'd have him look things over. And then let it all drop. She hadn't even brought the matter up with Christa yet. Until there was a viable fetus, until she knew whether the embryo had implanted itself in her uterus, and needed guardianship, she didn't want to jinx things.

Which was why she hadn't started on a nursery yet, either, other than the mental planning stage.

The microwave dinged. Her tea was done. Taking the cup out of the oven built in above her stove, she tentatively touched the edge of the cup to her lips. Sipping carefully. Hoping the lavender-infused liquid would calm the sudden clamoring within her.

But knew it wouldn't.

She couldn't let Seth's message go unanswered.

He was Seth. The only man who'd ever had the power to move her so completely. There'd been times when it had felt like the universe only held the two of them.

Besides, she'd been thinking more and more, about how much she'd love to have him in her baby's life. For the child's sake. Only if Seth wanted to be there, of course. But if he did want that, or even if there was a possibility that he might want that, she had to do everything she could to ease his way.

Picking up her phone, she typed, Yeah, I'm still up.

Seth had just about given up on getting a text back that night when Annie's reply came through. Picking up his phone, he went out to sit in a chair by the pool where he could relax in the late-August evening warmth, beneath a moon that pretty much lit up the backyard. He'd already had his swim. He was shirtless and in cotton pajama pants; the night air felt good to his skin.

He was going to text back, but hit Call instead before he could analyze the good or bad in doing so.

"Hey, Seth, what's up?"

He liked the way she answered the phone these days. *What's up?* Like they were old friends.

"I'm sending a document over to you," he said. "It's ready to go. I just wanted to give you a heads-up so you know what it is when you see it come in."

A text could have alerted her to the email.

"What kind of document?"

"It's a family history. The stuff that doesn't generally show up on all the genetic tests we did. You know, things like my grandfather having exhibited symptoms of ADHD his whole life, so he probably had it, but they didn't have that diagnosis back then. He was above average intelligent, but was not a good book learner and couldn't keep his concentration in one place very long, unless it was in a place that vastly interested him. And my great-grandmother played instruments by ear. Those types of things. My grandmother did our family genealogy back when that was just becoming a thing and she wrote what she knew about each person on the family tree. And then my father also put in his own notes." He wasn't generally so long-winded, unless he was in court, arguing a case.

And for some reason, that was what the conversation kind of felt like to him.

Though what case he was arguing, he didn't know. It wasn't like she'd refuse to read the email.

"Okay." She didn't argue at all. Or seem to give his gift all that much weight, either. "Thank you," she added as he had the thought. As though she could read his mind.

There'd been a time in his life when he'd have believed she could.

When he'd *known* she could.

"I was up with my dad today and he had this case…" He told her about it, in almost as much detail as his father had given, because she lived in that world. She'd get it. And when his recitation ended, he knew she got more than the case.

"That's why you're sending the family information," she said. "Thank you, Seth. You're... I just... thank you."

He heard the warmth in her tone and smiled.

His penis started to get a bit hard, too. Which, while wholly unwelcome, wasn't completely unexpected. Annie had always been able to get him going...even with just a particular tone in her voice. He sat forward, frowning. Would have ended the call, but right then she asked, "How's Randy doing?"

She'd loved his old man. More so probably since hers had died so young.

"He's great," he told her, leaning back again. Told her that his father was still working full-time. Still had a full head of hair. Still lived in the same house. And had still beaten him at the pool table that day, too.

"You just don't like the game enough to be that good at it," she said with a chuckle. And he nodded. She was right, of course.

There was rarely a time when Annie wasn't right. "So, how's your mom?"

Chelsea Whitaker Bolin had to be over the moon with news of the baby. After all, the woman who could have been heir to nearly a billion dollars had walked away without looking back because love meant more to her than any money ever would.

There'd been a time when a younger Annie had confided her hope that maybe his dad and her mom could get together, in a romantic sense. But while the two had been friendly enough, they'd each claimed their own private time with Seth and Annie, coming together only for major holidays. And when Seth and Annie had split, each parent had sided completely with their own child. Randy understood Seth's inability to see a cop as a wife and mother, after Seth had lost his own mother so tragically.

And Chelsea…she'd doted on Seth, adored him like the son she'd never had—until he'd hurt her daughter. Then she'd just quietly wished him well and walked away. Wouldn't answer his calls. And his Christmas card to her had been returned unopened.

"She died, Seth. Five years ago."

He swallowed, his gaze suddenly blurring. "She… what? How? Oh, God, Annie, I'm so sorry. I had no idea…"

"It's okay." He could feel her sadness. And hear it, too. "It was a freak boating accident. No one was at fault. She was out on a lake up north with friends she'd known since college. A girls' weekend at a cottage and…"

Her voice trailed off.

"Was anyone else hurt?"

"They all were. Mom was the only one who didn't make it, though."

He felt sick. Physically and otherwise, too. "Oh, God. I'm just so sorry…"

"It's not your fault."

"I should have known."

He should have been there for her. Chelsea was the only family Annie knew. To think…

He burned with guilt.

"I chose not to contact you," she told him. And it hit him. She'd said five years. He'd been married to Stella then.

He seemed to have a propensity for royally screwing up relationships. He might be a decorated lieutenant commander in the US navy, but when it came to women…he shook his head again.

"I'm so sorry I wasn't there, Annie. I loved Chelsea, too. So much." She'd stepped in and become a mother to him from day one. Not replacing the one he'd lost, but honoring her and being her own person in his life. Even as a young man he'd noticed the difference. And appreciated her sensitivity. That first Christmas he'd been with them, Chelsea had asked, *What was your mother's specialty? Your favorite holiday dish of hers?* And then she'd asked for the recipe and followed it exactly.

He swallowed. Wished he'd brought a beer outside with him. Life wasn't meant to be so tough.

"It's okay," Annie said softly, after a couple of

seconds. "Christa and Brett, her husband, were there with me the whole time."

Christa again. A woman he knew nothing about.

Except to know that he was grateful she was there for Annie. That she'd stepped up where Seth felt he had somehow failed.

And there it was again...the failure. During the last months of his marriage to Annie, that feeling had been prevalent in every conversation he'd tried to have with her. It got to the point where he'd get a pit in his gut every time he saw Annie's name come up on his phone. So much of that time she'd been deployed overseas and their face-to-face conversations were on the computer. Seeing her, needing her, being unable to touch her, to hold her, and then to have their conversations be in completely different hemispheres, as well...

That all had been hard. But when their life goals didn't mesh anymore, either...

Yeah, they'd done the right thing in splitting up.

And he'd done the right thing in giving her ownership of the embryos.

"You keep calling at night," Annie said, when, in other conversations, she'd have already said goodbye.

Was she feeling...this...this...*thing*...between them, too? Like they should be more than they were, but couldn't be?

He'd thought she'd be long and completely over him by now. But seeing each other again...and the whole pregnancy thing that would be ripe with emotions on its own…maybe they just had to stand strong and get through the rough waters. They were both navy. They knew how to sail.

"I call when I'm done with my responsibilities for the day," he told her, not wanting her to read any more into his attention than that. Whatever his struggles, baby and not, he wasn't putting them on her. Or building on quicksand. "And by the way, thanks for the referral to Kinder. We're going to put something together at the community center, a basketball tournament, to start, with law enforcement and teenagers teaming up to battle it out against other law enforcement and teenagers. It's got to start with a level of trust…"

He'd walked himself right into that one. He and Annie had once reveled in their shared trust in each other. It had been a key component of the wedding vows they'd written.

And relationships ended with broken trust. As they both well knew.

He waited for her to respond with a quick and professional goodbye. "You live alone?" she asked instead. Ignoring completely his reference to Kinder.

"Yes," he answered.

He didn't return the question. Couldn't contemplate whether or not there was another man in her life—one who would be stepfather to his child. That they'd be raising the child as their own—only needing Seth because he'd been the one to make embryos with Annie's healthy eggs. There was no room for the swirling emotions that thought unleashed. Jealousy. Anger—at himself, but the possible other guy, too.

But...wait...she'd said that Christa was going to be the baby's guardian. So that would mean...

Unless Christa and her husband were guardian to Annie and what's-his-name's kid in the event something happened to both of them.

"Are you seeing anyone?" Annie's tone was soft, almost curious. And...easy. Not like she was going through the rage of emotions attacking him.

"I see people," he said. "But not long enough for attachments to form. After things ended with Stella, I had to take a long look at myself and realize that I was the problem. I lack flexibility."

"You do, somewhat, sometimes, but you also take time to consider both sides, Seth. And...when you can, you eventually come around." The immediate response settled some of the storm inside him. If only because it made him curious enough to get his head out of the darker places. "Even now, Seth...you don't want children, they aren't your dream anymore. You were happy thinking the embryos had been destroyed. And yet you had the flexibility to allow me to have what I needed."

That was different. He'd owed her. Paying debts didn't count.

"And your work at the community center. No way

that office is conducive to you doing your job the way you like to do it. You want the walls lined with law books in the event you need to refer to them. But you make do."

He did prefer pretty much any other office he'd ever worked in to the one at the center. But… "Anything I need to reference is digital now, and I have my computer with me."

"How about your plans for dinner on Sunday? You said your dad was going to grill out, but he was on the case and you thawed a pork roast and had it ready when he got home…"

He didn't realize he'd gone into so much detail in the telling.

"You're flexible, Seth. You look at what's in front of you and find a plan to make it work."

He did like plans. She had that much right.

"So…you seeing anyone?" He returned her question.

"Absolutely not. A relationship is the last kind of complication I need right now."

She said she had to go.

And as he told her good-night, the knife was back in his gut. Sad that "complication" was what partnership had come to mean to her.

Though he didn't necessarily disagree with her assessment.

Still, the world was filled with happy marriages and successful partnerships. So maybe those were just for some people. A certain kind.

Maybe neither he nor Annie fit the bill. Maybe they'd been doomed from the start and neither of them had had a chance...

Beer inspired thought.

And he was completely, stone-cold sober.

Chapter Eight

Annie didn't speak to Seth again after that Wednesday-night conversation for almost two months. Fall had come and was slowly melding into winter—though, for California, the change wasn't all that drastic. She'd gained a pound or two, but nothing overtly noticeable yet, and woke every single morning with a rush of excitement, feeling like a new woman. She was no longer a one-person family. She and her baby were joined and had started their lives together. And while she worried sometimes about all that could go wrong, about being a good enough mother, especially since she would be a single parent, she also felt the most incredible sense of peace. She'd done the right thing.

She'd heard that Seth and Ben Kinder had held a successful one-day basketball tournament at the San Diego Community Center.

She'd cried when she'd read the family history information he'd sent. Randy's notes—they'd sounded like the talker he was. The tone rambled a bit, but he always had a valid point. And Seth's more acerbic but also to-the-point additions had clearly given her every intimate mental and physical health detail they knew.

Still, that night—well, in the early morning hours—she'd emailed Seth back, confirming that she'd received the document and had been able to open it, and added a thank-you.

He hadn't responded. She'd checked her email more often for a few days, waiting to hear from him, but hadn't. The disappointment had been crushing.

And then she'd seen the blessing in his stopping whatever it was that had been starting up between them. Had been thankful. Because they had nowhere to go together. Not as two people. They couldn't be friends…not after all they'd been to each other. Even in the few interactions they'd had recently, it had become clear that they had too much intimate knowledge in a heart sense, knew each other far too well to ever just be friends.

But she was holding on to hope for them as parents of a third person, as opposed to two people. Holding on maybe more than she should be, with her imaginings of different possible ways Seth could play a role in the baby's life in the future. Somehow those little scenarios she played out for herself had become her go-to anytime she got scared or worried, anytime she felt a hint of a cramp and feared she might be losing the baby.

Anytime she started to wonder what she'd do if she didn't carry the baby to term.

And every time, those daydreams calmed her enough to gather her resources and go on.

A couple of weeks after that last conversation, Seth had texted her. Just checking in, he'd said. Wanting to know that everything was good.

That she was still pregnant, she'd translated.

She'd told him she'd let him know if things weren't status quo. Hadn't he believed her?

He didn't trust her. The knowledge became fact to her with a clarity that had her texting him right back.

Status quo. And I will keep my word to you. I will let you know if anything changes.

She hadn't told him she had no morning sickness so far, something that was good news to her, but also had her worried that she wasn't having a normal pregnancy.

And she'd spent that night alternating between smiling that her welfare, or that of the baby, mattered to him in the here and now, not just the past, and crying for the here and now and the past they'd lost. Never, in a billion years, would she have figured, when they'd gone with hearts full of hope and determination to create those embryos, that they'd be birthing one separately.

And yet, what a miracle every moment was that she had her baby growing inside her.

After that first text, Seth texted every couple of weeks, just to ask if everything was good.

And she answered back that all was fine.

She didn't know what they were doing there. Touching each other while pretending that they weren't?

Because it seemed as though they were keeping in touch.

And with no real purpose attached.

The one-month check had been quick and done. There'd been a blood test. Other things, too, because with implantation they watched carefully. But during that second-month check, after Dr. Miller examined her, she told Annie she wanted to have an ultrasound done and then they'd meet up in her office.

Fear took a hold of Annie the second she heard the words. No good could come of "I'm calling for a test right now, to see more clearly what is or isn't happening inside you, and then we have to talk."

"Tell me what's going on," she said, maybe a little too much like a police lieutenant used to giving orders than a pregnant patient. She had another ultra-sound scheduled, but not for another couple of weeks.

"I just want to get a look," Dr. Miller said as she turned with her hand on the doorknob.

Still sitting on the examining table, the paper sheet wrapped around her lower body, Annie shook her head. "Do you think something's wrong? Is the baby…"

Alive?

She couldn't ask.

The doctor dropped her hand from the door, walked over to Annie and squeezed her wrist. "The baby is growing," she said. "I want to get a look at positioning."

Okay. Positioning. She knew, vaguely, what that could mean. Not in detail. Not really. But enough to know that if it was wrong, it could be fixed.

Positioning, she could deal with. She got dressed to walk down the hall and climb onto another exam table and bare her not-quite-flat belly. As she lay there, feeling the cold gel being smeared across her belly, she could feel the tension building in her. What if something was still wrong? The moment was at hand… They were going to know if there was really a baby growing inside her.

Would they find a heartbeat?

And if not, then…

A vision of Seth's face came to mind, the way he'd looked when he'd first opened the door to her at the grungy office all those weeks ago. His blue eyes had seemed to devour her. The gaze seemed to pull her into the room toward him. And because she'd had such an important purpose for being there, she'd let herself be reeled in.

His shoulders had seemed huge to her, filling out the white short-sleeved shirt of his uniform in a way she'd never seen. As though he worked out a lot more than he had when they'd been together—though they'd both done their three hours a week in the gym. And the bars on his chest, the colors were different, and more plentiful. He'd made lieutenant commander. He hadn't said so, but she'd seen the rank designation.

And…oh, God…

"Here we are…" the technician, a young Black woman named Shanice, with a gentle touch and sweet smile, said as she moved the handheld camera device across Annie's stomach. She pointed with her other hand to a screen right in front of both of them. Annie saw masses of gray shadows. Light and dark. "Here's the head…"

She didn't see a head. She saw waves moving.

"Here's the spine…"

Oh. There. Those shadows that looked like notches? Shanice was measuring and clicking and noting as she worked, while Annie stared at the masses in front of her.

If there was great cause for alarm in what was on

that screen, the technician wouldn't be calmly measuring, would she?

Of course, she wouldn't.

But…that meant… Annie swallowed back tears. She wasn't going to be weak.

A foot was pointed out. Annie latched onto it.

And thought of Seth. Thinking he'd be interested in deciphering every one of those shadows. In the olden days, that was. He'd have *been* interested. The two of them, they'd created that foot.

Her baby had a foot.

She had a baby.

The technician clicked, touched a computer screen off to her right, typed.

The pregnancy…it was real.

It was real!

Oh my God! It's real!

"And here we go… Let's see if we can get a heartbeat…"

She held her breath. From what she'd read, twelve weeks was far enough along…she was only eight…

And there it was.

Rapid. But steady. Louder than she'd have thought.

Tears sprang to her eyes as relief made her weak. She didn't give a hoot about that, either.

"Wait," she said, reaching in her side pants pocket for the tiny, handheld recorder she'd purchased for this purpose and pulled out of her purse as she'd entered the room, she pushed the little button and recorded that blessed heartbeat sound.

A dream from long ago.

She and Seth had been so certain about their plans when they'd created those embryos.

And there she was, more than a decade later, making the dream come true.

She was finally going to have her baby.

But she was doing it without him.

The tears that clouded Annie's vision weren't all happy ones.

Seth was just finishing lunch with James and Donovan, two of the other attorneys in his office, when the ringtone sounded. *Annie.*

Throwing some money on the table, he excused himself, said he'd make his own way back to base, exited the restaurant—a favorite of naval officers along the pier—and strode along the sidewalk parallel to the ocean until he reached a bench. Sitting, he pulled out his phone.

If she'd lost the baby, he needed to be able to talk to her in private.

Turn the volume all the way up.

She'd sent a video.

Thumb to the volume button on his phone, he did as she'd instructed and hit Play.

Then he felt himself starting to shake.

He couldn't make out much on what was obviously an ultrasound, something she'd obviously gotten from the tech, but he heard what she'd shared with him loud and clear. The baby's heartbeat.

She'd managed to grow a live fetus with a beating heart.

From their embryos.

Her child, though.

The video ended and he hit Play again. And again. Just kept watching. Listening. Elated. And grieving for all that wasn't to be.

Unsure what to do with himself. How did you feel such contrasting emotions at the same time? He didn't know whether to laugh out loud or howl in pain. Just sat there, excited and grieving at the same time. Fired up and burning out.

He couldn't put the phone away. Couldn't get up and resume his life. He had no idea who he was anymore, other than a lieutenant commander and lawyer with the US navy.

The child he'd helped create with such surety was coming to life. A decade after he'd thought all possibility destroyed.

He'd helped make that embryo. It couldn't have happened without him. He'd been vital to the process. And he'd done it because he'd believed that he wanted that child more than anything else on earth. That he wouldn't be complete without it.

And there it was, heart beating strong and sure, without him.

But when he thought about being the man he'd been…he shuddered in a new way. No happiness as an accompaniment. He couldn't be the guy who hurt those he loved.

Couldn't go back when he already knew his shortcomings. He was great at loving when it all was going in such a way that he was comfortable. But the second things got uncomfortable—when they didn't go as planned and he couldn't find a way to fix it— he bailed. Emotionally, if not physically.

He was forty years old. Was beyond the point in his life where he thought sleepless nights with a crying baby would be an adventure.

And had long ago reinvented his life plan to focus on a career that could require long-term travel with little notice. He wanted to be *that* guy. Was comfortable with him. More important, he slept well at night in that man's skin.

Time passed. He didn't know how much. At some point he quit hitting Play. Went back to the text message box and typed, Congratulations, but didn't hit Send. Wasn't ready to move forward. To take a step in any direction.

Congratulations was far too distant. Too uninvolved.

And anything more was too much.

And yet…he wasn't just a sperm donor. Everything about him stilled as understanding came to him. He hadn't donated his biological component; he'd helped create his own child.

He'd never contemplated donating his sperm for someone unknown to him to use. Or for anyone to use outside of him building his own family. He thought it was great that other guys did that, for such great purpose, but it wasn't his calling.

He was a man who felt biological attachment. Responsibility. Hence, the family history packet he'd sent to Annie weeks ago. The guardianship he'd offered to help her set up.

He was also a man who'd created embryos with the woman he loved for the sole purpose of them raising a family together.

They'd failed together. They weren't going to be a family. But he was still going to have a biological child in the world.

The dichotomy within him wasn't just going to disappear. Those embryos had been made out of love.

He'd connected to them as he would to the fetus they eventually brought forth. And the child that came into the world from there.

That heartbeat came from him, too.

He'd grieved for those embryos when the marriage ended. When he'd thought they'd been destroyed.

And now, in the midst of joy for Annie, for the child, there was a completely different kind of grief. The loss of his part in the child's life.

He had no role.

Back at the text, he hit Call instead of Send.

Annie got up from her desk and shut the door of her office when she saw Seth's call coming through. She'd come straight from the clinic to the office and had been hit with a burglary case the second she'd walked in. By the time she'd sent two detectives out to investigate, an assault call had come in and her third detective was on that. She hadn't even seen Christa, to tell her about the ultrasound.

"Hello?" *Seth, what's up?* Just wouldn't come out.

"Hi."

Emotion thickened the space around her.

His and hers. Always there. Neither of them knowing what to do with it. Or about it.

It had been that way at the end of their marriage, too. They'd had to get out or suffocate from it.

"You got the text?" Clearly, he had. He wouldn't be calling out of the blue. Not with that kind of timing.

"We did it." His tone was warm. And odd. She didn't recognize it. Or know what to make of it. Didn't know how to proceed.

Tearing up, she turned away from the window in the wall that also housed her door, making her visible to the office beyond. Turned her back on the view of the office she supervised.

"Yes."

"I...want you to know... I couldn't be happier, Annie. I...this is good. I'm glad for you."

His obvious sincerity, the thickness of his voice, the difficulty with which he'd evidently said the words, swept through her with a swift wave of tingles. Alerting her to what she already knew.

Seth was deeply affected by the use of the embryos. She hadn't thought the whole thing through—not where he was concerned. Herself and the baby, having a baby alone, their future—she had all of those covered. In triplicate. But Seth?

She hadn't ever let herself think about him. The coping mechanism that had seen her through their divorce, the lonely years afterward while she was making a career for herself all alone without his support, when he'd remarried, when her mother died... the way she got through was to not think about Seth.

And even if she'd known that Seth's life would be upended by her use of their embryos...she'd have made the same choice. He'd chosen to leave her rather than try to live with her as she was. Maybe he'd have been proven right. Maybe his fear for her safety would have ended their marriage anyway. But he hadn't even tried.

When she'd chosen to go into law enforcement rather than social work, their dream had ended for him. It hadn't ended for her. She still wanted to raise a family. Those embryos were her only chance to have a child of her own. And it wasn't as though he'd wanted them for himself.

So…she'd gotten what she wanted. And now she had to be accountable to the fallout—Seth's discomfort. She owed him a debt of gratitude. She wanted to do what she could to ease his way, as she forged her own.

Chapter Nine

"I'm still struggling to believe it's real," Annie told Seth. He'd been hanging silently on the line since his proclamation of joy on her behalf. And then she added that the ultrasound hadn't been planned, that she'd had one scheduled at thirteen weeks, not eight.

Figuring out how to include Seth's emotions on the fly wasn't easy. But he liked facts. Those things he could grasp. Decipher. Plan around.

"The test was unplanned? Did the doctor suspect something was wrong?" Leave it to him to home in on the part that had left her feeling most vulnerable. Unsure.

The part she hadn't yet processed at all. The baby was alive. Had a healthy heartbeat. The rest of what had been said in her meeting with Dr. Miller after the ultrasound…she was only letting it seep in slowly. A bit at a time. It was how she kept panic at bay. A thirty-eight-year-old police lieutenant, soon to be a single parent, couldn't afford panic.

"With implantation there are things they watch for, in particular. One is the size of the baby…they need to know that it's getting the proper amount of nutrients for healthy development…" She repeated what Dr. Miller had told her almost verbatim. And tried to ignore the tightening in her throat and chest. She would not cry. Nor was she going to borrow trouble from the future, when it might not even exist to borrow from. Everything might be just fine.

Seth's silence didn't deter her. She knew he'd wait to hear all the facts and then say what he had to say. "She was surprised at the thickening of my waist, and what she thought could be baby positioning. Could just be I'm eating too much, but she wanted to get the baby's measurements, to monitor growth and determine placement in the womb."

"And?" he asked after she'd been silent a full thirty seconds.

This was where it got baffling. "The baby's position is perfectly normal. The torso, spine, and arm and leg bones measured just a tinge below average for eight weeks, which, to Dr. Miller, meant that everything's normal there…"

"Okay." She could hear his tone lightening and had to cut him off.

"She wants me to have another ultrasound." Annie relayed the facts that had been playing with her mind ever since she left work.

"Why?"

"My placenta is a little enlarged. They only heard one heartbeat, but…there's a possibility there might be a second baby behind the first. And that if it's there, it might not be alive. That second embryo might have implanted, but not made it." She had a healthy heartbeat. There might only be one child. No reason to mourn yet.

"What happens then?"

"Often times it's reabsorbed." She was still trying to wrap her mind around the whole concept. "And there's also a chance, because it's so early on, that a second baby is completely hidden, but alive. It's rare, but possible. The technician only saw one fetus, and found only one heartbeat, though she apparently was searching for a second of both. Apparently hearing a heartbeat at all isn't all that common with the Doppler at eight weeks. The doctor had been surprised that we got such a strong one."

"There might be twins?"

Yeah. And she wanted them both. As badly as

she'd wanted one. She didn't want a second baby to reabsorb.

He made no sound.

"She said she could do an internal ultrasound that would be able to pick up both heartbeats, if there are two. Or I could wait and have another test like I did today…in another couple of weeks."

She paused, and when there was still nothing from him, just kept talking. "I asked her if there was any health risk in waiting and when she said there was not, I decided to wait. I just don't want anything in there poking at my uterus this early on. I know it's illogical, and not at all medically based, but as long as there's no risk in waiting…"

His silence was expected. And disappointing. Had she made the right choice? What did he think, damn it?

Her disappointment was unfair.

"Have you thought any more about guardianship? About getting the paperwork done?"

He was there. Not engaging in her medical choice. But he was there.

"I haven't talked to Christa yet."

"You should do a trust, with guardianship named there. That will take care of your estate and protect your heir's assets. I can handle it for you."

"Okay." She didn't have the energy to fight with herself about whether or not she should involve him further.

And maybe she still needed him a little bit, too. Deep down inside where the woman who'd sworn her whole heart to him still lingered.

"It would be best if we can sit down and go through it all. I'll need to list all assets and designations. I'm free this weekend and could make the trip up. Get a room by the beach. I haven't run on the beach in Marie Cove in years."

She hadn't run in years, actually, getting all of her workouts in at the gym. But in the olden days, they'd run together. On the beach, and off.

The idea of him being in Marie Cove made her heart leap. Excitement welled within her. And she knew both were wrong.

"What are we doing here, Seth?"

"Making a trust."

"Seth…"

He didn't answer. Reminding her of too many times in the past when silence had been his answer to the impasse that had grown between them.

She was deciding whether or not to call him on it, to spew her fear in the form of frustration, or just tell him goodbye and hang up, leaning more toward the latter, when he said, "I don't know my role."

"What?" She'd heard him. Needed him to express himself with more words. Or at least ones that made sense.

He had no role.

Unless...did he truly want one? Not just in her dreams, but...seriously?

She couldn't let hope grow. Most particularly now that she knew there really was a baby, that another human being would be affected by all of the choices she made from then on.

And...what if there were two babies?

"I'm not a sperm donor, Annie. I committed to something when I contributed to those embryos. Or even, I committed a part of myself when we created the embryos. I heard that heartbeat and..."

She didn't fill in any blanks for him. Just waited. Mostly because she had no answers to give him. And had no idea what he really wanted.

She only knew what she hoped to have from him someday.

It wasn't right to ask for it, though. She'd asked for those embryos, no strings attached.

Besides, she didn't want to guilt him into anything.

"We started on a plan and the plan's coming to be, but I've been wiped out of the picture."

Only because he'd wanted it that way. Her heart rate sped up.

"Do you want to be in the picture?"

"No!" He sounded so certain her heart lurched. Maybe it cracked a little. "But I don't want to be out of it, either."

Settling back in her chair, Annie felt like herself

for the first time since she'd been in the doctor's office and heard the word "ultrasound." She was, ultimately, a problem solver.

And they had a doozy.

"What do you have to offer?" she asked him, ready to listen to him. Not just think of herself. His confusion was understandable, based on their bizarre circumstances. And there was no doubt in her mind that her child would benefit from knowing him.

"I don't know. We know we don't work as husband and wife."

He'd get no argument from her on that one.

"We didn't want to bring any child into what we'd become," he said.

"Agreed." Which didn't preclude some kind of arrangement by which he was a part of the baby's life. That, however, could only come from him.

"I've got nothing," he told her.

"Nothing to offer?" She'd known she couldn't get her hopes up. Funny, how hope didn't always listen to reason.

"No solutions," he said. "And maybe nothing to offer, based on us, our past. I can't be in, which means I'm out. But…for now…how about I focus on something I'm good at and get your trust set up?"

He wanted to do it.

She wanted him to do it. "I'd like that."

"And you're good with this weekend?"

She'd been planning to ask Christa to go to Mission Viejo, the town between Marie Cove and LA, to go nursery shopping. But her friend had called that morning and said the following week would actually work better. "Fine."

He was going to hang up. She knew. And said, "Seth?"

"Yeah?"

"Just so you know...your role...if you figure something out, I'm open to hearing about it."

"We can't be who we thought we'd be when we started down this path."

"I know. Believe me, I feel as strongly about that as you do."

"Just so you know, I fully realize that it's my fault," he admitted. "That I'm the one who messed it up for us."

He hadn't said so at the time. And it took her a second to be able to take a breath. And not to have the sound of imminent tears in her voice. "Thank you for that."

"But also, so you know... I'm still that same guy."

She nodded, and knew she had to be honest with him. "Even if you weren't, Seth, it still wouldn't work. I trusted you implicitly. With my life. And to have my back. To put me first. Just as I put you first. Once that kind of trust is broken, there's no going back."

"I'm sorry, Annie. I never meant to hurt you. Never would have believed I could."

Which was part of what made it all so difficult to get over. Even a decade later. But she'd hurt him, too, by becoming someone different than she'd presented herself to be. Even if she hadn't consciously made that choice.

A cop with a gun at her hip? Never in a million years would she have seen that for herself when she'd joined the navy in order to get a college education in social work. She'd been scared to death of being deployed to a war zone and having to fight for her country. She'd have done it—*had* done it, as it turned out—but she'd never seen herself as having the strength to do it without debilitating fear. Never would have believed she'd be so good at it.

Still…she'd expected Seth to at least try to understand. To give their marriage a chance.

Instead she'd come home from months away to have him tell her he'd become friends with a female JAG. He hadn't started anything with that other woman, but at the time, the distinction hadn't mattered all that much.

Because while Seth had been growing more and more distant with his disapproval, she'd grown close to someone else, too. Someone on deployment with her who'd watched her blossom under an unexpected assignment. Who'd cheered her on. Been proud of her newfound strengths and success…

But that was then. In her present…she'd just heard her own baby's heartbeat.

"Let's leave the past in the past," she said. "And take the rest one day at a time." Because the pregnancy was one day at a time. Every night when she went to bed, she celebrated another day of keeping the baby inside her. "I just wanted you to know that, as far as the baby goes, I'm not opposed to considering options if you have a way you want to be... involved."

"I'm already involved, Annie," he said, his tone a mixture of frustration and...was that conciliation? "I created those embryos with the full intention of being a father. I didn't realize the ramification of that until all of this. Probably still haven't fully realized it, but that heartbeat..."

"Yeah. It's pretty cool, huh?"

"Better than cool. You're sure you're feeling okay?"

"I feel fine. Normal." No sign of morning sickness and Dr. Miller had said that it wasn't cause for worry. Some women just didn't have any. She was fine, either way.

Seth's silence started to make her tense, though. "So... I'll see you this weekend?" she asked.

"Saturday. Midmorning. You want me to come to your office?"

No. She still wasn't telling anyone other than the captain and Christa. Not until she passed the first trimester, at least.

"Come to the house. If things get too weird, we can head out to a coffee shop or something."

"How about if you come to my hotel? I'll let you know where I'm staying. I'm sure there's some alcove off the lobby or something where we'll be able to converse privately."

His idea was much better.

Safer.

And made her sad, too.

Hard to comprehend that it was wrong for Seth to be in her home.

Seth made his hotel reservation—a luxury place with private beach access—only after ascertaining that he could also reserve one of the small, glass-walled conference rooms. He had no intention of heading out to the beach with Annie or heading out alone while leaving her in their meeting space—but the idea that they were on the ocean...made the meeting seem...better. The ocean had been one of "their" things.

The rest of the week he focused on business, getting through a record number of files for him in an effort to keep his mind so occupied there'd be no time for extraneous thought. He'd saved the video Annie had sent on his phone but didn't access it again. And wouldn't let himself ask questions for which he had no answers.

The plan was one day at a time and he stuck to it.

That created a cache of pent-up energy. Early Saturday morning he spent an extra half hour at the gym, but he was still het up with anticipation as he set off for Marie Cove. As soon as his ten o'clock meeting with Annie was over, he was planning to spend the majority of the eighty-degree-sunny October day at the beach. Running. Swimming. Maybe even renting a board and getting a little amateur surfing in. Whatever it took to fall into bed tired that night.

Sunday morning, he'd work up the initial trust paperwork for Annie, have her look it over, and head back south to get the formal document drawn up, send it to her for notification, and be done with it.

Done with his part in the embryo process? The growth of the baby?

The question nagged at him as he drove, but he refused to give it enough attention to come up with a response. One day at a time.

Having dropped his bag in his bedroom, Seth was already set up in the conference room down a series of hallways on the main floor by the time Annie arrived. He'd texted her the room number as soon as he'd checked in, and changed into brown pants and a short-sleeved off-white business shirt minus a tie, before heading to the meeting.

He was an attorney handling business.

And something else. But since there was no description, no apparent definition or action required of that something else, he left it alone. Determined not to let it hijack the day at hand.

Classic case of burying his head in the sand. He got it. Accepted it. To do otherwise, to spend time letting his brain take him in circles, served no good purpose.

And his heart...he'd learned a long time ago to expend that energy on compassionate listening with the sailors who came to him, during volunteer work at the community center, and, of course, with his father. Anything more tended to end up in hurt—his own, and others'.

Some people were just that way.

No way he'd ever intentionally hurt a baby. But what if the kid wanted to be something Seth never saw coming? Something that would put her in even worse danger than daily police work? Like fighting global virus terrorism or tracking down serial killers?

Would Seth support their child on that quest?

He was still shaking his head in response to that internal interrogation when Annie showed up in the opened doorway.

All buisness, like him, in gray pants and a silky-looking lavender button-down, tapered short-sleeved shirt that hung just low enough to cover the belt at her waist, she didn't hesitate when she stepped in to greet him. Standing at one side of the four-chair table, he started to reach out a hand—his typical

greeting as he welcomed clients in to a meeting—
but pulled back and hid the action by reaching for
the papers he'd just laid out as he'd wanted them. In
order of the information he needed to get from her.

Whether she'd meant to run her fingers through
her short, blond hair or was pulling back her own
hand, he didn't want to know. Those big blue eyes
looked his way, their gazes locked for a second, and
then it was done.

She was nothing but professional as she sat perpendicular to him—her back to the ocean—when
he'd purposely taken a side chair so that she could
have the one that was full-on ocean view. She'd always loved the water as much as he had. Had drawn
strength and pleasure from it.

So her message in seat choice was that she wasn't
there for anything but work? Had plenty of strength
for the task at hand?

Or he wasn't as in control as he'd thought and was
reading too much into every little nuance, trying to
squeeze far more out of seconds than actually existed within them.

It was no surprise that Annie came prepared,
though. The financials she laid out were in docu-
mented order, with a cover sheet. He looked them
over, impressed.

And he felt proud of her.

He had an equally lucrative portfolio, but he
guessed she'd had to work harder for hers. His work

had been largely in an office, and he got pay grade bumps and excellent benefits just for staying in the service.

"Those are all copies," she told him. "You can destroy them when you've finished setting up the trust."

Taking a moment to compose his thoughts, to remember that they were together on official legal business, that she was, in essence, a client, he flipped through everything again. Then again, starting with the first asset, he went through all of them with her, clarifying where needed, making certain that he had full understanding of where everything was. Verifying that she had full ownership of all of it and had given executorship to no one else.

"And how do you want it laid out in the trust?"

"Everything goes to my heir," she said, her hands in her lap as she gave a small nod. "Or heirs."

A jolt of energy went through him. *Heirs.* More than one. Because there might be two within the current situation. With his head still facing the documents on the table, he glanced up and over at her. He didn't mean to connect over anything that could be perceived as personal, and quickly broke eye contact.

But not before he'd landed back in time for long enough to get his emotions going. He swallowed. Turned a page. And another.

Annie could very well be having twins. *Their* twins. Multiple births had been a possibility they'd been counseled over when they'd decided to go straight for embryonic implantation over months and possibly years of continuing to try to get pregnant.

The trust was to be set up with her offspring as sole and equal heirs. That made his job simpler.

"Because this trust is being designed to serve you anytime in the future, even if you live to be a hundred, the assets will all go to who you name on the trust with you, but because of the possibility of your heir being underage when the trust is settled, you'll need to name a trustee. I'd recommend that whomever you name as guardian also be the trustee, so the child isn't caught between possible warring factions, but that's just a recommendation. You can choose to set this up however you'd like. The guardianship can be done simply by you writing a letter that we'll file with the trust…"

"I haven't spoken to Christa yet, regarding the guardianship…"

Her married friend whose husband would then step in as father of the child. Or children. The ones created from Seth's embryonic component.

"But…in any case… I'd like to name you as trustee," she said, and he glanced up fully that time. Meeting her gaze head-on. "It can stay purely legal," she said quickly, her expression lined with…doubt.

Because she doubted him? Was afraid to put more on him than she should?

There was no doubt in him as to her voice—her

tone had been authoritative. Just her silent plea to him had held a lack of confidence.

And there'd been no hesitation in her response, either. She'd already chosen him as trustee before she'd come to the meeting. The idea came to him with a certainty he didn't question. A certainty that buoyed him.

"I mean it to be purely legal," she amended. "It's just…in legal matters… I trust you implicitly, Seth. I'd feel better knowing that if something happened to me, you'd be in charge of protecting my baby's future."

Not in charge of the baby. Just of the future. The money. The provisions. The college fund. Her home as an asset.

In those areas she trusted him implicitly. Not in the others. Not anymore. He'd had that trust and had destroyed it.

His throat tightened with an ambush of emotions he couldn't sort out. Or express. Jumbled bits of despair, of guilt, of regret.

Was still needing to be right where he was, doing what he was doing.

He blinked.

And, in answer to her request, he nodded.

Chapter Ten

"I'm going into work for a couple of hours but… we could meet someplace later for dinner, if you'd like…"

Standing at the door of Seth's makeshift office for the day, saying goodbye until the following morning, Annie heard the words come out of her mouth and knew they were wrong.

No matter how badly she might need to make things right with him, she and Seth could not go out for dinner together.

Because there was no way to make things right.

They could move past what had happened years ago. And that was all.

They hadn't moved far enough past to allow a casual dinner, though, just the two of them. What would they talk about? How could they possibly have real conversation between them without getting themselves into trouble?

He knew how she thought. She knew him, as well...

"I've already got plans," he told her, almost too quickly. As though, after the awkward silence following her question, his words had been tripping over themselves to be said.

She nodded. Relieved.

Disappointed.

And beginning to suspect that she hadn't just failed to consider and understand all of the ramifications for Seth in her decision to use their embryos. She'd had a wrong read on herself, as well, thinking that she could see him, carry his child, and not fall back into some of the old feeling between them.

The great love with which they'd created those embryos.

Or what she'd thought had been a great love. Her continuation of her parents' kind of love.

He had plans. That was good. Better for everyone.

With a woman? Had he brought someone with him for the weekend? Was she out at the pool right then, on the beach, or up in his room, waiting for him?

It would probably be best if he did have someone with him. Not many women would turn down a chance to be with the decorated and oh-so-sexy navy lieutenant commander for the weekend.

The thought brought her an instant flash of Seth naked, his tight buttocks moving up and down on top of her, blowing everything out of her mind except the ecstasy he always brought her. Even in the end.

They'd never lost how good they were in bed.

She had to leave. They were both just standing there.

Him probably ready for her to be gone. And her wondering if they'd still be so incredible together.

She'd had some lovers since him. None had come close.

But Seth had married again. He'd had to have found great sex to do that.

"I…wasn't going to ask, and definitely not before tomorrow, when we finalize things here, but…maybe it's best I give you the night to consider…" He didn't sound like himself…unsure like that.

"What?" Anything had to be better than the road her mind had gone down.

"I'd…like to be present for the second ultrasound, if you could be okay with that. Not as the father," he added hastily. "Just…it seems that if there's going to be a second child to consider, I'd like to be present for the news, to process information as it comes, rather than you telling me by text and then us trying to hash things out over the phone."

She could ask Christa to go to the appointment with her so she wouldn't be alone. She wouldn't. But she could. And they didn't have to hash anything out.

He'd asked her to keep him apprised of pertinent information, as per his Parent Portal contract. Period.

"I know how private you are, and like to keep your business to yourself, but…twins? That's not something you hear every day."

"My appointment is for a week from Wednesday. At nine in the morning." Right in the middle of the week. "I'm sure you have to work." She didn't offer to make a change.

Partially because when he'd offered to come be with her for a test that was making her extremely nervous…she'd taken a step off the high wire for a second.

"I can drive up in the morning and be back by lunchtime," he said easily. "I don't want to burden you with my presence or push my way in, in any way. I'm just trying to be responsible to the situation," he said.

She thought about that. Was still thinking about it when he added, "Taking things one day at a time."

That was what they'd decided to do.

"Because we're never going to be anything together," she said aloud. No matter how much she'd burned to climb his bones, or have him climb hers, just a moment before. "But you do have biological, though not legal, interest in the child."

"Or children," he affirmed with a nod.

"Then, okay. But… Seth, is it really necessary for us to meet again tomorrow? It's not like, if I die tomorrow, we'll have any need of this trust. Take your time to work it up, I can look it over by email, and then when you're here for the ultrasound, we can arrange to have it signed and notarized."

She couldn't spend the rest of the day and night thinking about seeing him again, right there in town, the next morning. There wasn't enough work to occupy her sufficiently and make her not yearn for him. What she needed was time.

Hopefully the next ten days would be enough.

At least to get her through that morning's visit.

And then there might be months before their next interaction. Time to figure out a way to be able to be around him without pain. Or longing.

Assuming she managed to carry the baby to term, that was. If not, there'd be no more interaction between them.

The baby was the only reason they were in contact at all.

When Seth agreed to her plan, she gave him one last thank-you, accompanied by a weird-feeling smile, and bugged out.

Before she could make a total mess of things by leaning in to kiss lips she'd been dreaming about for ten long, lonely years.

* * *

Final trust papers ready for her signature on the seat beside him, Seth arrived at The Parent Portal twenty minutes early on the Wednesday of the ultrasound. He'd been up before dawn, had been to the gym, to the office, and spent most of the drive up on the phone with Captain Kinder, trying to sort out a truancy report discrepancy with one of his kids from the center, and discussing another community center activity that would involve entire families. The basketball tournament, in which Seth and the captain had both played, had been a beginning. But if the idea was to build trust between police and troubled kids, they had to do much more. Seth's clients trusted him. With him involved, they were more likely to participate.

And the truancy issue—well, that was the other side of what the youth task force was designed to do. To help set a kid straight rather than throw him in the criminal justice system. This time, Seth believed it was going to work. One case.

But it was one of those things that you chipped away at on a case-by-case basis.

One case at a time.

One day at a time.

He was about to hear the baby's heartbeat for real. Not by recording. To see arms and legs, a torso and head.

He was about to meet his child. Maybe even two of them.

But wasn't going to be a father.

And was no closer to figuring out how the child's existence affected his life. There wasn't a plan for a guy giving up his rights to the embryos he'd created, and then coming face-to-face with the done deal. Or ear-to-heartbeat-recording as the case might be.

And even if there was, emotions, morals, ethics, sense of right and wrong…they didn't all track the same from one person to another.

The second he saw Annie's shiny, dark blue, unmarked four-door sedan pull into the lot, Seth was out of his car. He hadn't wanted to come in his navy whites, but he had an appointment that afternoon with a sailor who was deploying and leaving in the middle of a rancorous divorce, so he couldn't be late, and he hadn't known how long his time in Marie Cove would take.

"You ready for this?" he asked as soon as Annie was in hearing distance. In light brown pants, a tan shirt with long, puffed sleeves, brown, slightly heeled shoes, and with the shirt hanging over the gun at her waist, she looked every bit the police lieutenant. Until he glanced up and saw the shaded look in the big blue eyes framed by those spiky blond bangs.

Of course, she wasn't ready. How could she be?

He started to hold out his hand to her, knowing she needed to take it, and quickly slid it into the pocket of his pants, instead.

"It's good to see you," she said, falling into step beside him, a foot or more between them.

He started right in then about his conversation with Kinder, talking to her about his truant client who'd been home caring for a sick grandparent who'd lose custody of her if Social Services knew she was sick. The ailment wasn't terminal and was, in fact, almost healed. He kept talking about it because he had nothing real to say to her right then.

And because he was nervous as hell.

It didn't happen often.

Pretty much never, that he could recall. He was a "take charge, deal with it, or make a new plan" type of guy.

Being at the mercy of Annie's choice, medical science, and a tiny unborn fetus growing at its own pace, or deciding not to do so, was not coming easily for him. Being at the mercy of anyone's choices, when they were difficult for him, had turned out to be his nemesis.

One that he avoided at all costs.

Until he'd heard that heartbeat.

He'd thought they'd have a minute or two in the waiting room, time for Annie to maybe clue him in on what to expect, but the second they walked in the door, a woman who'd been standing at the window behind the receptionist nodded at Annie and appeared almost immediately at the door leading to the exam rooms.

She introduced him to a woman named Shanice, saying that Seth was her ex-husband and the baby's biological father. Until that moment, he hadn't even thought about how his presence would be described. He'd been to The Parent Portal with Annie several times in the past. Had once been as much of a patient/client there as she was.

Shanice nodded as though both titles were commonplace and continued on down the hall. Seth followed the two of them, shoulders back, the bars on the breast of his uniform displayed with pride. He was the biological father.

He finally had a role. One that his sperm had handled with aplomb.

Seth wasn't feeling quite so pumped a few minutes later. He stood awkwardly off to the side while Annie got situated on the padded exam table, pulled up her top and undid the fastener at her waist to push the pants and her panties down to her pubic bone.

Showing the top of the dark but not black curls that he'd once been so intimately acquainted with. They were still there.

Of course, they were.

But looked so...familiar.

The jolt that went through him, landing in his penis, had him embarrassed and a bit ashamed, too. He was lucky to be there at all. Annie didn't deserve to have her trust betrayed by him lusting after her in a medical situation.

But seconds later, as Shanice put some kind of gel on Annie's slight rise of a belly and started moving the hand-held camera around, he wished he could get back to lusting after her.

Annie hadn't said a word to him since they'd walked in the room. He didn't dare look at her. Leary of what he'd see. And if she was looking at him, afraid of what *she'd* see. She always had had a way of knowing what he was feeling before he did.

Something about their relationship he hadn't liked.

It was good to remember, lest fantasy and time reframe things to have him thinking that maybe he'd made a mistake. Maybe they had. Maybe they could be something in each other's lives again.

"Here's the torso…" Shanice's tone drew out and stopped. She'd been using an arrow on the screen to point, but was moving the camera on Annie's belly, instead. Seeming to Seth to be studying the screen more intently.

"Excuse me," she said. "If you don't mind, I'd like to get the doctor in here…"

Seth stepped forward as Annie half rose. "What's wrong? Is the baby alive?" He'd never heard such panic in her tone. His calm, rational, always-the-one-who-said-it-would-be-okay Annie sounded as though she was ready to bounce off a wall.

And his own sense of reason took over. He placed a hand on her shoulder and rubbed gently, while also helping her to lie back, as they both looked at Shanice.

"The baby's alive and growing," the woman said, sounding more perplexed than worried. Turning back to Annie, she quickly moved the device in her hand, adjusted a knob, and a sound very familiar to Seth filled the room.

"The heartbeat song," he said aloud, when he'd meant to speak to himself. Annie glanced at him just as he glanced down at her, and when their eyes met, he held on. Just for then. That moment in time. In that room.

They'd get her through it, he promised silently. Whatever it was.

She didn't say a word as Shanice took a quick leave. Just kept looking at the now quiet monitor bearing a still photo of the last image Shanice had shown them, with an occasional glance at him.

"You know your baby is alive," he said, starting to worry that he'd made another promise he couldn't keep. He had no idea what the technician had seen that she'd thought needed a doctor's attention. And no way of knowing if he had anything to offer that could help Annie in any case.

Gaze toward the screen, she nodded.

"A healthy heart is paramount. That and the brain. Anything else they can fix," he told her, wondering if maybe the way he was feeling was how his father felt when he rambled so. He sure as hell hoped not, since Randy Morgan had been rambling nonstop ever since Seth could remember.

They could fix the heart, too, he amended silently. And sometimes the brain.

There was a reason he listened more than he spoke.

He liked to get his thoughts in order before he put them out there. Better all the way around.

Oh, God. Annie didn't deserve a setback now.

And the baby...the embryo they'd created...nothing could happen to it. That was all. They'd been so certain they were making perfect children for a perfect family...

He barely had time to sense movement from the table by which he stood, before Annie's fingers found his, curled around them, holding on.

She didn't look at him. Didn't say anything.

He kept his mouth shut, too.

But he let his fingers wrap hers into an old but still familiar cocoon, and vowed that, somehow, he'd get her through whatever was to come.

Chapter Eleven

The room was small, its light muted, with barely enough room for the chair that sat along the wall. Yet Annie didn't feel closed in. With Seth there, looking all official in his uniform, as though daring anything or anyone to try to bring danger to them, she felt... safe. Her mind was creating an illusion to help her get through whatever was coming next, but she allowed herself to exist within that fantasy space for the two or three minutes it took for Shanice to return with Dr. Miller.

Seth stood back as the doctor entered, though Annie noticed he and the doctor nodded at each other. In recognition? They'd only met a couple of times in the past.

Her fingers missed his touch. She focused on that lack, glommed on it as the camera once again moved across her belly. She couldn't see the screen now. Wasn't sure if Seth could. She wasn't looking at him. Instead, she'd closed her eyes. Was remembering him standing beside her. Holding her hand.

For that second, he'd been the man he'd once been in her life.

She missed him.

"I see." Dr. Miller broke the silence that had fallen. "Right." Annie figured she was speaking about something Shanice had relayed when she'd gone to collect her.

Had the doctor been in another patient's room? Was whatever they were looking at urgent enough to interrupt an exam?

No. She'd had a glimpse of Dr. Miller at the desk in her office when they'd come down the hall.

"I'm just going to try to move the baby a bit," Dr. Miller said, applying very slight pressure to Annie's stomach. And then said, "Okay, let's try to get a heartbeat."

A tense few seconds followed, with Annie staring at the two medical personnel crowding the space. She'd held on for about as long as she could. Panic was welling.

Movement sounded off to her right. Slight. And then big, warm fingers enveloped her cold hand lying on the edge of the table, and she could breathe again.

She didn't look at Seth. Didn't dare. She couldn't fall apart. And she couldn't fall into him, either.

There were three people with her at that moment, but when she left that room, she'd be alone. Handling the situation as a single mother had to do.

Her choice.

She'd made it.

The knowledge gave her an odd kind of strength. Seth's fingers seemed to have cleared her mind enough for her to come out of the black abyss of the unknown and back into herself.

"And...there." Dr. Miller turned just as a sound hit the room. Not as loud and strong, but unmistakably a heartbeat.

"There *are* two of them," Shanice exclaimed.

"And both have healthy heartbeats," the doctor said, turning to smile at Annie as she moved away from the screen.

*Da dum, Da dum, Da dum...*she heard the sound. Could see the screen now, though her eyes were blurred with moisture, but couldn't make out two separate bodies.

She needed to see them. To have proof that...

And then another sound hit the room.

Da duh, da duh, da duh... Definitely different. To her ears, it was completely different. "Like different voices," she said, her own voice cracking. Two heartbeats.

Two voices.

Two babies.

She was having twins!

And Seth slid away from the table.

What was he doing here? As the ultrasound ended and they were ready to leave the room, Annie had asked Seth if he wanted to go with her to meet with the doctor. To hear about what was next.

To hear the actual results of the ultrasound, which hadn't yet been discussed in any detail.

He'd said yes as though he'd given her question any thought. He hadn't.

But he should have done.

As the doctor showed them to side-by-side chairs in front of her desk, he could barely lower himself into his seat. They'd been in the office before. As husband and wife.

He knew how it looked, the two of them there together again, and it wasn't that.

Wasn't ever going to be that.

He sat out of respect for Annie. She didn't deserve a scene. Most particularly not when he'd been the one to ask to be there at all.

He started to clarify his reason for being there, briefly, when Dr. Miller started to speak.

He was present as the biological father, not the dad to the baby…babies…two of them…twins…

Sweat pooled between his shoulder blades. On his neck.

"…the way they're positioned, one of top of the other…" He heard more words than those, but didn't compute them. Maybe they'd come back.

Annie was having twins. From the embryos they'd created together. He kept hearing the same words, as he had been from Annie's first visit to him almost three months before, as though a mere repetition of basic facts was going to serve some purpose at some point. Get him somewhere.

They didn't.

"We're going to need to watch closely," Dr. Miller continued, speaking mostly to Annie, but looking in his direction a time or two, as well. As yet she hadn't said anything directly to him.

She'd know that he'd signed away his right to the embryos.

Had Annie told her anything more about his presence there that day? Warned her?

"It's not unusual for one baby to be larger than the other, but I'm a little concerned about baby number two's small size…"

"So, what do I do? Are there some other vitamins? Something that will encourage growth? Do I sleep on my other side, or…"

The doctor shook her head as Annie, sitting slightly forward, started in with the questions. Annie's intent look, her attention to detail when he'd been off lolling around about where he fit in the picture, smacked him upside the head.

Him being there wasn't about him.

"What are the next steps?" The calm he heard in his tone settled over him. He was the fact guy. The one with the clear head.

That was his role. That was why he was there. It all started to play out for him in an order that made sense.

"We're just going to keep a close watch on things," Dr. Miller said. "I'm telling you what I saw, and what we hope to see over the coming weeks, in terms of growth. There's nothing for you to do." She was looking at Annie as she said that last part. "Just continue like you are. Take your vitamins. Eat well, as we've already talked about, and get plenty of rest."

"Are you worried?" Annie asked, seeming not to relax one iota at the doctor's words. "What do you think are my chances of carrying both to term?"

His heart jolted. He didn't think they needed to be going there. Though he was the one who planned for the future. Who insisted on a plan.

"I think you have a good chance," the fifty-something-year-old Dr. Miller said, her lab coat seeming to give the words more weight. "Twin births do tend to go into labor earlier, and with your age…we'll be watching more closely when you get to your third trimester. We might adjust your activity level. But for now…" She shrugged.

Seth was reassured, but looked at Annie to ascertain her emotional state. If she needed more information, they'd continue to sit there.

She was nodding. Still intently focused. But her face didn't look quite as pinched.

And then the doctor mentioned that she wanted to schedule an amniocentesis, talked about the reasons why, possible genetic defects for one, as well as the risks in having the test at all, and Seth's agitation started up again.

His genes could be creating peril inside those little bodies. A slight risk of miscarriage came with the test to find out. There were two sacs, but a way for one needle insertion to test both.

Annie's skin had paled, her cheeks sucked in with tension again.

And he knew he wasn't done yet.

The test was serious. And potentially uncomfortable, too.

No way was it right for him to sit back and have Annie go through that alone.

He was, after all, a biological contributor.

And he loved the woman who'd have to deal with whatever he'd contributed.

Annie left the doctor's office in a daze. She was having twins! More work. And more joy! A second child even if she only got the one pregnancy. Excitement rippled through her every time she relived the seconds when she recognized her second baby's heartbeat as unique and different.

And...the heartbeat had been fainter. That baby was too small.

Great joy and a huge worry, all meshed together, left her emotionally exhausted and unable to slow her nerves down enough to get herself centered.

And then there was Seth...walking silently beside her, his black dress shoes crunching against the gravel in the parking lot, his face not quite grim. But close.

What the knowledge of two babies was doing to him, she could only guess. But knew it wouldn't be good.

Twins were...special. Like icing on the cake, but more like cake on cake. Two cakes.

Before the morning's news he'd been dealing with the loss of one baby. Now he was losing out on two...

She had an entire, brand-new future spreading before her. A family.

Thank God, she was finally going to have a family!

And Seth had...nothing. Except his job. Volunteer work.

And girlfriends along the way.

"I have a favor to ask," she blurted. "Work-related." She'd thought of him a time or two over the past twenty-four hours, in terms of a case, but had specifically and stridently told herself she wasn't going to mention it to him.

She knew it was wrong to pull him any further into her sphere. Had consciously made the decision not to do so. And yet…something drove her to reach out to him in the only way she felt she could.

"Because of the work you're doing with Ben Kinder…with the youth task force…" He'd jumped right in. And with good success.

"What do you need?" He stood a foot away, sort of meeting her gaze. Looking more toward her forehead than her eyes, but dipping down briefly, too.

They'd reached her department-issued, unmarked sedan. She unlocked the door, hoping he didn't see that her hand was shaking.

She was having twins! Two babies. Two cribs. Two needing to eat at night…

He was going to leave. Go back to San Diego. And deal with his lack of participation in the wealth all alone…

"There've been a series of burglaries, mostly here, but we think they're tied to a couple in the LA area, as well. We've got a fourteen-year-old kid who's sitting in detention waiting to be arraigned, but he insists he's innocent. That he's been set up to take the fall for a couple of rich kids he knows…" The whole story came pouring out. About the string of burglaries, where home invasions had happened through the same kind of windows. Only cash and video games were stolen. Nothing that could be traced, like credit cards or guns. No electronics. Standing there with

Parent Portal patients arriving or leaving around them, she explained how Emilio knew the kids because he'd been delivering pot to them for his older brother. Always to different places. How his brother had told him he had to keep doing what they wanted because they needed the money. And how his brother had driven him to LA to make the drop-offs.

"Sounds like, if anything, the brother is in on it…"

She shook her head. "My detectives already went that route. Big brother has never met the teens in question. He says they approached Emilio down at the beach because they knew his brother had connections. Emilio has been the go-between all along.

"The two teens he names, both male, are white, with wealthy, divorced parents. Both sixteen. Neither has any kind of record or history of wrongdoing. They admit to buying pot from Emilio, but that's all."

"And the LA connection?" Seth was frowning, but with concentration. It had been a long time since she'd seen him at work. Since she'd thought about how much she admired the passion he gave to his job. No one worked harder than Seth did.

"Scott Thomason, one of the teens, visits his father there twice a month, both visits coinciding with recorded pot deliveries and burglaries."

"Did you get search warrants for all parties, to see if the video games turned up?"

She nodded. "They didn't."

"And I'm guessing no surveillance camera footage or prints were found from any of the scenes?"

"There's some footage, blurry… We can only make out movement from one body…"

"One body, not two."

"It's just in a corner of a neighboring camera. If there were two perps, the footage wouldn't have shown it. Not from that angle. And there were no prints or anything we could get off the windows themselves. They're a common window used by many of the builders in the area."

"How'd you come up with Emilio as a suspect?"

That was part of what was making the case hard for her. "His older brother came in, gave himself up as a dealer, pot only, because he was worried what he'd gotten his brother into. He heard about the burglaries, put together that they coincided with Emilio's deliveries, and was afraid his kid brother was heading down the wrong road."

Big brother cared. Annie had no doubt about that.

"So, what do you want from me?" His words wiped out all thought for a second. She looked up at him, unable to answer.

And then remembered what they were talking about.

"A fair shot," she nearly blurted. "For Emilio. The teens' parents have already called in high-dollar attorneys. Emilio can't afford anything but a public defender. In all of my time questioning him—after my detectives had had their go first—Emilio never came off his story. He says he didn't do it. And that we have to believe him. Either the kid is a pro already, and working me...or he's counting on me to help him. My detectives are still going through things, looking for anything that could prove, definitively, who's behind the burglaries, but if they don't come up with anything new...the best I can do is try to get this kid a top-notch attorney. I know you can't represent him in court. But...like with your volunteer work at the center...if you could take a look at things...at least talk to him so he knows he's being heard...give him the same high-priced-lawyer edge that the other kids have, it would level the playing field some."

Or give Emilio the impression that he was getting more of a fair shot.

Not that that was necessarily going to change his outcome. But...

"He reminds me of my dad at that age," she said, wishing the sun shining down on them would warm the chill in the air enough that she'd quit feeling like she was ready to shiver. "If anyone had given my dad any hope that he'd be treated fairly, he'd have been off the streets long before he was..." Danny Bolin had been a good kid in a rough neighborhood. He'd done some minor things—stealing food mostly—but had been judged harshly because of where he was from. And as a young kid, with the pressure of needing to stay alive, he'd compromised his ethics a time or two, hanging with a gang for a while, for safety more than anything else. But he'd never hurt another life. Or carried a weapon.

"I'll talk to him," Seth said, and while she knew real relief for Emilio, she also was swamped with guilt. She never should have called in her "dad" element. Seth knew more than most how much her father's early years had affected her career choice. She'd played an emotional card and that hadn't been fair.

It was beneath her.

Unlike her.

But then, she didn't know who she was, sometimes, when she was with him. The past, the years in between, the person she'd become...they all got confused, like balls in a bingo wheel, when he was around.

He was her ex. The man who'd hurt her more than she'd ever thought possible for one person to hurt.

He'd been the love of her life.

He was the father of her children.

Biological father, she amended as Seth was saying... "I can't see him this afternoon, but I can drive back up tomorrow..." Letting his sentence float, he walked off in the direction of his own car. He was just going to leave? Had she pissed him off?

She wanted to tell him that it was okay, she'd manage without him. That she'd been wrong to say anything. That she'd find another way. And saw him head to the passenger side of his car, instead of the driver's side. He wasn't leaving. He was reaching for a folder.

And she remembered the trust. They'd emailed back and forth, and the final version was ready for her notarized signature. He had the folder outstretched as he made it back to her, saying, "Have this signed and notarized by tomorrow and I'll get it from you when I come back and get it filed."

He was all business. Not mad at all, just…so distant. After what they'd just shared. She wanted to call him on it, but she just nodded. Gave his hand a squeeze he didn't return, unlocked her car door and lowered herself in the seat, turning, with one foot still on the ground to look up at him.

"Thank you."

He nodded.

"For Emilio. But also for this morning. Having you there made it…easier."

He nodded again. Said nothing, and then turned to go.

Giving her neither a "you're welcome" nor a "goodbye."

Annie closed the door of her car and sat watching him in the side mirror until he'd made it to his vehicle, with tears in her eyes at his aloneness. He wasn't hers anymore. And she didn't want him to be.

But he still had the power to move her. And she still cared about what happened to him.

Maybe life wasn't as cut and dried as she'd thought.

Chapter Twelve

He loved her. Still in shock from the revelation, Seth topped the speed limit all the way back to San Diego. The hour-long commute, doubled with the return visit, meant two fewer hours in the day to get things done. And he'd be doing a repeat performance the next day, as well.

He loved Annie.

Of course, he did. Made sense. She'd been the other half of him, able to know his thoughts sometimes before he did...

Love didn't die just because someone changed professions. Maybe it didn't ever go away. No matter how the people carrying it screwed up.

Did she know how he felt?

Miles flew by, road signs glinting under the sun, blue skies overhead sending promises of a bright day, and he couldn't seem to be a part of it. He was outside looking in. On the day.

On life.

On the lives of his children.

Twins.

He'd been a spectator to the miraculous revelation. Needed to be.

And yet…how different would it have been if he and Annie had still been together as planned when their embryos came to life?

Signaling, he crossed to the left lane, sped past the vehicles beside him, and then reentered the right-hand lane. Thought of Annie up in the middle of the night, a baby in each arm crying for diaper changes and feedings. Her needing to be up for work the next day. And almost thirty-nine years old by that point.

With him in San Diego, having all the free time in the world, in a house filled with emptiness.

There had to be a way he could help out, from outside the family.

Did she love him? Made sense that she might, at least in some measure. Loving each other had never been a problem. Living together after their choices had taken them in different directions…that had caused the strife. They'd each had needs the other couldn't fill.

Could he ever be around Annie without needing more from her? Knowing more about her than a casual bystander, or even friend, would know? Like he'd known just when to hold her hand that morning. And when to let go, too.

She was having twins. And had no other family in her life.

Unless…had she been in touch with her mother's family? Had they come to Chelsea's funeral? How would that have gone, Annie seeing grandparents she'd never met, during her time of deepest mourning? She'd have been cordial to them, as was Annie's way.

But had she let them in? Would they be helping to raise his children? *His children.*

Because, call it what you wanted, those twins were half him. No matter who raised them. If his genetics could be responsible for any birth defects, they were equal contributors to all of the good in the makeup of those babies, too.

Ten miles until his turnoff and he couldn't go fast enough. Had to pull his foot off the gas pedal lest he risk seriously breaking the speed laws.

Twins. He and Annie had talked about multiples when they'd done all of the research on implantation. He'd thought the idea kind of cool. Until she'd brought up the whole "two babies up all night needing feedings" part of it.

Back then, he'd thought differently about a lot of things.

At forty, he knew himself a whole lot better.

Twins. With a mother who wore a gun on her hip, who put herself on the front line every day when she went to work. Maybe not out on the streets all day anymore, but still there, in the thick of it. Dealing with dangerous people. Working in a profession that some attacked just for doing what they did.

Working in a profession where statistically, the chance of dying on the job was greater than most.

She could go to work and not come home.

Seth knew what that was like. Didn't want it for those two little shadows on the screen. Couldn't deal with it himself, again, on a daily basis. Not after he'd answered that door once before. Saw the looks on the officers' faces...

He'd reached his exit.

Was bringing home a mind filled with answerless questions. And a very real sense that he couldn't just walk away from them.

He had to talk to Annie. Really talk.

They had to figure this thing out.

Annie didn't sleep well. Between being excited about the twins and worried for them, concerned about her thirty-eight-year-old body having sufficient ability to carry them healthily to term, wondering about genders and names and handling it all, nervous about the nightly feedings and whether or not the cribs should be side by side or across the room from each other, ditto for the portable cribs she'd have in her room for the first couple of months at least, and being completely unsettled where Seth was concerned—it was a wonder she'd slept at all.

But never, not once, did she doubt her decision to use those embryos and have herself implanted.

She'd had dinner with Christa. Made the "twin" announcement. But hadn't asked the detective to be guardian to her offspring. Not yet. Caring for two at once…that was double the ask…and she needed time to think about it all. There was no doubt in her mind that Christa would be honored by the request and agree to it, willing to step up in a time of tragedy, to love Annie's children. Her friend had already told her about a hundred times that she'd be there to help with anything Annie needed. Anytime.

But Christa didn't want children of her own, and two of them? Annie just didn't want to overburden Christa, in the event Annie really did lose her life to the job. Or to any of the other millions of things that took human life. Taking on twins alone…

Telling herself she wasn't dressing with any thought of seeing Seth at work that morning, Annie still chose the black pants and matching short jacket that she generally saved for days that included lunch with the captain, or some other such thing. The pants were a little snug across her belly, but with an adjustable button and the white silky tunic she wore under the jacket hanging down over the pants closure, she was able to expand them enough to get the job done.

She'd put a little more gel in her blond bangs, and to give the rest of her cut the lift that made it look more like a style rather than just hair sitting on her head. Added a touch of mascara in addition to the eyeliner she always wore, and dusted a hint of beige eye shadow, too.

Not for Seth, but just because she was starting the first day of her new life. Or so she told herself. And wanted to believe. She had to take this thing head-on from the very start. Had to know she was enough.

And had to know, as she had her ex-husband in her office for the first time ever, that she could show him how well she'd done. How right her choice to enter law enforcement had been for her life.

After all, that choice—and his reaction to it—had cost them their marriage and family.

She'd been jittery since she'd gotten out of bed that morning, but as she stepped into the station and rode the elevator up to the second floor, she felt more like herself. In control.

Ready to take on whatever presented itself throughout the day.

Emilio, who'd been formally charged the day before and was out on bail in the custody of his older brother, and said brother, Juan, were waiting when she got to the squad room, on her way to her office.

Offering them something to drink, she showed them into an interrogation room and then went to get the soda and coffee they'd requested. By the time she was back with them, she'd had a text from one of her detectives, telling her that Seth had arrived.

In navy whites again. With a worn leather satchel under his arm. God, he looked so good to her. Drool-worthy good. And apparently Britney, her most junior detective, thought so, too. The way her head was cocked, and the look in her eye, the smile on her face, as she talked to Seth, said something Annie didn't want to "hear." No way was she okay with one of her employees flirting with her ex-husband.

Period.

So maybe she was a little brisk as she took charge of Seth, cutting off her detective midsentence, and led him back to introduce him to Juan and Emilio. On the short trip down the hallway she didn't meet his gaze and kept a minimum distance of a foot between them. She thanked him for coming, in lieu of hello, and asked him if traffic had been bad on the drive up.

His response—"It was fine"—was about what she'd expected. She hadn't expected his gaze to linger on her, though, as she turned to face him just before opening the door. For a second there it was like he was eating her up—sexually, but the connection was much deeper than that, too. Almost spiritual.

Her system went on autopilot and let him draw

whatever he needed from her. Getting something unexpected in return.

It all happened so fast she couldn't describe it. But as she made her way back to her office, after telling Seth to text her when his meeting was through, she was no longer jealous of Britney Jorgenson, which was a good thing because the woman was one hell of a good detective.

She and Seth had had a monogamous, intimate relationship. It hadn't worked. Their marriage, their partnership, had ended. But a thread between them, a connection, had survived.

Right along with the embryos they'd created.

She couldn't define it, couldn't put words to it, but whatever it was that connected them wasn't something anyone—not even her or Seth—could sever.

He texted twenty minutes after she'd left him. Shook Juan's hand and squeezed Emilio's shoulder as the two left, and then, still in the doorway of the interrogation room, turned to Annie. "You got a minute?"

She had a full day's work waiting, and two new cases on the docket, but after he'd driven the hour up to help her out, no way she could refuse him.

Leading him back into the room, she shut the door. They'd have a lot more privacy there than in her office, with its wall of windows overlooking the squad room.

Something about his demeanor told her she was going to want the privacy.

Plus, she didn't need her detectives and assistants gossiping about her locked in her office with the to-die-for-handsome sailor.

Still standing by the door she'd just closed, she faced him.

"What's up?" Something to do with Emilio, obviously, but why that personal look? Was he about to tell her someone on her staff had made a mistake? Or was he convinced that Emilio was the crook and playing her?

"I want to be guardian to the children."

She stared. Felt her face stiffen, as though no blood was traveling through it. Knew she'd heard him correctly, but couldn't figure out where he was coming from.

"You said that you'd be open to conversation when I figure out my role, and that's it," he continued. "You're the parent. The children are yours. I signed away my ownership of the embryos and I don't regret any of that. I'm glad that you're having the chance to live your best life…"

He always got talkative when he was presenting a case… The thought occurred to her, distracted her, as her stomach dropped, and her heart started to pound. He didn't present his cases until he'd thought everything through. Was sure of himself.

This wasn't just a chat. What he was suggesting…

"I'm not intending that we co-parent. Only that, in the event that something would happen to you, I become their guardian."

Yeah, she'd gotten that part. He wanted their kids?

Her heart leaped and she tried to calm herself. Put a hand back on the doorknob for steadiness.

Did this mean...

She shook her head.

No. She and Seth couldn't get back...

And there'd be no way he'd suggest such a thing.

But since she'd seen him again, she'd been impressed several times with a certainty that she wanted him in their lives...down the road. Wanted for her kids to know their father, to reap the benefit of having him in their lives...

Her breathing slowed.

"Instead of Christa," he said. "I'm sorry if you've asked her since we last spoke about it, if she and her husband are already on board, but I feel pretty strongly about this. Most particularly since we now know there are two of them."

Why the number mattered, she wasn't sure, but she wanted to grant his request. With such enthusiasm that she held back, checked herself. Didn't correct his mistake regarding Christa's marital status. Didn't point out that she was a cop widow.

Wondered if maybe Seth was why she hadn't already asked Christa.

She couldn't fall back into the person she'd been,

couldn't get hurt again. She had to make certain that before she agreed to something, she was doing it for the right reasons.

"Taking on two at once?" he said. "I know that's a huge commitment for someone who never really expected to have to do so, someone who's a friend, but not family, like Christa. There's a good chance some resentment could arise when things get particularly tough, as they undoubtedly would if your family suddenly increased by two demanding little people. Especially if that friend has kids of her own to provide for. I, however, am the other creator in this process. Those children biologically belong to me. I would take on the responsibility with the same type of commitment to those children as you have."

Not really. She'd wanted to be a parent to these embryos. He didn't.

But would a guy who felt no parental pull even make the suggestion?

"Furthermore, this guarantees that I would always be permitted to step in on their behalves, if you weren't there to do it. Otherwise, if another guardian would have the rights to our children, and if they were suffering, I'd have no legal recourse for helping them."

What was he doing just now?

And...what would she be doing to her children if she turned him down?

"You sure you don't want more time to think about

this?" she asked him. "The only time I've ever seen you give up anything was when I pushed the emotional trigger left from your mother's death. One of our children could also choose to live in harm's way."

"I'm positive." He reached into the satchel he'd carried in with him—she'd figured it contained his laptop so he could look up anything he might need to know pursuant to Emilio's case or California juvenile law. Pulling out a folder similar to the one she had ready in her office for him to take back to San Diego, he handed it to her. "Here's the tentative paperwork for you to look over. If you agree with everything there, we'll need to have separate attorneys handle it for us, one for you and one for me, but we should be able to get this done in pretty short order."

He wasn't kidding.

Or planning to change his mind, either.

"I wasn't there for you, Annie, but I will be there for our children if needed. Until the day I die. No matter what they take on. No matter how much worry or stress they cause. I'm their father."

Annie took the folder, careful not to let her fingers touch his. He was getting too close. Making her want to start relying on him again, and that couldn't happen.

Him in the lives of her children, occasionally, that had been a pipe dream. One she still wanted and could have lived with.

But him legally bound to them... What would her

fickle heart make of that one? And how much pain would it end up costing her? And possibly her kids?

If they both made it to term.

Looking up at Seth, finding calm in his gaze, she just stood there, looking for answers that she knew she couldn't take from him. She had to come up with her own. Based on what she knew, not on how he made her feel.

But, oh, God, them together again, just in terms of the kids they'd so desperately wanted...

No.

That was the danger. Right there. That. Her trying to make them soulmates again. In any fashion.

It wouldn't be fair to any of them. Least of all the babies.

And there was no way she was going to tell Seth he couldn't have access to them.

"I'll call an attorney," she finally told him.

Because, for the children, it was the right thing to do.

Chapter Thirteen

The amnio was scheduled at fifteen weeks, right in the middle of December. Seth hadn't seen Annie since he'd been down to meet with Emilio and Juan five weeks before, but they'd texted each week. Him asking how she was doing, her saying fine.

His guardianship of the twins was set up, filed, and done. The trust was established. And charges had been dropped against Emilio, too. Seth had built up what his argument would be as defense attorney, proving that all evidence was circumstantial. He'd pointed out various areas where there should have been proof of the thefts if Emilio had been guilty—some extra cash showing up somewhere in his life or sales of video games—and in a call with the DA had persuaded him to let the kid go.

Annie had thanked him in a quick email from her work account and told him that her detectives were still pursuing the case.

He'd filed the email away in his personal folder.

Telling himself that they were doing fine, that they'd figured the whole thing out where they and the fetuses were concerned, he went back to his usual routine, working out, reporting to the base, volunteering… And in the evening, he'd taken up reading.

About twins. Twin gestation. Multiple births.

Just so he'd be prepared in case he was called upon. And he did some research on chances for genetic abnormalities in later-in-life pregnancies, and prognoses, as well.

He'd had Thanksgiving dinner with his father, thinking of Annie on and off all day. She hadn't said what she was doing for the holiday. He hadn't asked. Their personal lives had to be off-limits. It was the only way it was going to work for them. And he hadn't told Randy about the coming babies, either. Randy wasn't going to get to be a grandfather—there was no point in rubbing his nose in it.

He'd wondered, again, if maybe Annie was with her maternal grandparents or other extended family, but didn't try to find out. Not his business.

But if they were in her life…wouldn't she have listed them as guardians from the beginning?

He'd texted on December 1, telling her he'd like to be present at the amniocentesis if that wouldn't bother her, or make it harder for her.

She'd sent back the response he was getting a little too used to seeing: Fine.

That little four-letter word was beginning to irritate him.

His problem, not hers.

At home on Monday night, two days before the scheduled procedure, he was having a beer and going over some legal briefs, doing a bit of follow-up case law research for a meeting the next morning, when the soft jazz tune played from his phone. For a second there, with his focus on a government legal matter, he forgot what the sound meant.

And then remembered with a burst of tension.

Annie.

Calling, not texting.

"It's Seth," he answered, somewhat stupidly, as soon as his fumbling fingers could get the phone out and open. "What's wrong?"

If she'd lost those babies... Grief grabbed him, started tearing through the muscles in his heart.

"Nothing. Just...can you talk for a second?"

Nothing. It took a moment for him to absorb the cool relief coming over him. Nothing was wrong.

"Of course," he told her, sitting back at his desk, gathering his wits back about him. It was just because he'd been so absorbed in the work, keeping track of all of the threads that had to come together for the argument to carry weight, that he'd overreacted.

He waited for her to talk.

Silence hung on the line. They'd perfected that one, hanging wordlessly around each other.

Because there was still so much they could say to each other—most of which couldn't be said between them. Not anymore.

He could care, but he couldn't be warm or get closer. He could have compassion but had to keep it on an intellectual level.

Neither of them would survive anything more. In retrospect, maybe they'd been fools to think that Annie could use their embryos and have the world continue to spin normally on its axis.

"Talk to me, Annie." He couldn't just leave her hanging there until she hung up. He was afraid she would and then he wouldn't know what she needed.

"I should probably just go."

"Probably. But tell me first why you called."

"I'm scared. I still haven't told anyone but my captain and Christa about the babies. I've just been wearing loose shirts, and with it being colder, my thigh-length sweater as a coat and that adds another layer."

"You're afraid to tell people you're pregnant?" He knew that wasn't what she'd meant. Had no idea why he'd asked the inane question. Maybe to buy himself a second while he settled back down after her *I'm scared*. It wasn't his place to go into immediate rescue mode.

Not with her. Not anymore.

And yet everything in him had clenched when he'd heard those two words. *I'm scared.*

Annie didn't get scared. And certainly didn't admit it if she did.

"I'm afraid of the amnio," she said. "I know it's necessary. I know, statistically, there's less risk with waiting until the fifteenth week… I know I'm making everything worse by thinking about it so much. I really should go."

"No. Wait." He couldn't leave her there alone, not like that. "Maybe if we just talk about it a minute or two," he said. "Get everything out so that it's not just rattling around inside your head…"

"You're the only one who really knows what this means to me, Seth. And… I'm scared to death I'm going to miscarry. I know the percentages are small, but it does happen and…"

"You've got extra embryos." The words flew out without thought attached. He heard them. Groaned silently. "I'm not making light of any loss that could occur," he quickly stated. "And I hope and pray that the babies come through just fine, as they most likely will. I'm just reminding you, Annie, that your entire life isn't wrapped up in just one chance. Look bigger. Further."

As he said the words, more flowed. Because he knew her. Knew how, when she couldn't find her peace, she tended to focus on a problem until it seemed like the whole of her world, in her effort to handle it.

"Look beyond for a second," she said softly, and he had to swallow. Hard. He used to tell her that. When one or the other of them was going to be away and she'd be afraid that something would happen to prevent them from coming back together, or she'd be focusing on how horribly lonely she'd be, he'd tell her to look beyond. Look beyond the separation. Or, when bills piled up, to look beyond the money worries. Look beyond... There was always more life out there. More good that would come.

When grief overwhelmed her after another period came, he'd tell her to look beyond. They had another month right ahead, another ovulation coming right up. More chances to try.

Look beyond just long enough to get out of panic mode, and then she'd be able to deal with whatever she faced.

He'd learned the coping mechanism as a kid, when either of his parents had been called out on a dangerous case. And then, when the worst happened, after his mother had died...he had to look beyond that time in his life, that moment when he'd answered the door, that emptiness, toward his own contribution to make the world a better place.

"The more you focus on the fear, the greater it will grow," he told her.

"So why couldn't you focus less on the fear, Seth?" The question came softly. "Why did your fear have to end our marriage?"

He'd asked himself the question more times than he could count. Never found an answer, just kept asking. Until, eventually, he'd quit asking.

"I don't know." But, sitting there, his emotions raw, maybe he did. "Would you want every day to be like the day before an amnio?" he asked her, thinking out loud as much as anything. "Would you want to work that hard within yourself to not think about what could happen? And then still have moments of panic when the fear took root behind your back and slugged you one?"

"No."

Everyone had fears. He imagined most every spouse of every law enforcement officer did. But in his case, having had the worst happen, having lived through the worst... He knew it firsthand so much more than most.

That knowing had taken root inside him. And could instantly flower into paralyzing terror if challenged...

"Would you want to live with someone who did have that sense that every single day was like the day before an amnio where you were concerned?"

"No."

Vindication didn't bring any comfort. Just as going to therapy and being told that some residual emotional effect from his mother's death would always be with him, embedded in his psyche, and he couldn't be blamed for that, hadn't made him feel any better at all.

Still, there were always going to be days before amnios in life. You hoped they were few and far between, but they'd be there.

And when they were…

"How about I drive up tomorrow after work?" The question just felt right. "I can get a room, and we can have dinner someplace. Find distraction where we can—and you'll be with someone who's going through it with you, someone who knows your battle, for those moments when distraction doesn't work."

"That's not fair to you."

"Why not? You think I don't have something at stake here? That's my stuff you're growing there, too, you know." He tried for light. It fell flat, but he was still glad he'd tried when she chuckled.

"It'll be time out of time, Annie. It's very clear we both know the score where you and I are concerned. These past couple of months have shown us that. We made the right choice ten years ago. We don't belong together. But we can do this together. We can get you through a tough test as you work to bring our children into the world."

His words hung in the silence, but he stood

with them. Weeks of just one text, checking on the babies, had paved the new way for them. She was the parent. He was the background support, called into action only when needed. Mirrored his job, too. It was what he was good at.

"Annie? If you'd rather not, it's not going to hurt my feelings. The offer stands if you want it."

"What do you think about just staying here?" she asked. "I've got a couple of extra bedrooms, one with its own bath. The worst is when it's the middle of the night, the city's asleep and the house feels so empty, like I'm the only one in the world…"

It sounded as though she'd had many of those nights. All since the pregnancy? How much had she been suffering alone?

She'd made no mention of her maternal biological family. The Whitakers. So he didn't mention them, either…

Stay at her house? She'd just invited him to spend the night with her. Sort of. He'd never even been to her house. So hard to grasp, considering that they'd once chosen everything about their home together. How much of her stuff would he recognize?

If he went, that was.

"If you'd rather not, that's fine," she said now. "Maybe it wasn't a great idea. I apologize, Seth. Like I said, I have these bouts of fear, and absolutely don't want them to lead me into making mistakes…"

"I'll stay," he said, cutting her off. She'd made a

small ask of the support he'd promised her. He knew his role and was confident he could fulfill this one. Would not let her down again. "We're going to get you through this," he told her. "Salvaging those embryos, giving you the family you've always wanted… it's a way to make the past matter, in spite of how we ended up."

And he was getting too deep for their present. Feigning an urgency he didn't feel for the research still awaiting him that night, he rang off.

Finally feeling better about himself where Annie was concerned.

Seth had been right about one thing. Distraction helped keep panic at bay. And he had the ability to provide that distraction.

All day Tuesday, while she oversaw her squad and reported to the captain, the random thoughts, which had lately been consumed by worry over the babies, were occupied with thoughts of the evening ahead.

Thoughts of Seth.

And how she was going to keep herself on track with him in her home. Overnight.

She wanted him there.

Too much.

And that was the danger against which she must guard. As a law enforcement officer, she knew that the way to stay safe was to identify the hazard and protect against it. As long as you knew where the peril was, you'd likely be just fine.

It was the unknown jeopardy that posed the most threat.

Seth was not an unknown danger.

Not anymore.

And as a law enforcement officer, she didn't shy away from danger. She met it head-on and dealt with it. Defused it.

She was damned good at doing so.

And by the time she met Seth at one of her favorite restaurants down by the beach, with tables overlooking the ocean, she was confident that she could handle whatever risk being with him posed to her. Which then allowed her to take the benefit he offered.

A coping mechanism during the next twelve to fourteen hours, helping her manage her stress levels until she had the procedure that had become so problematic to her peace of mind.

She'd worn her black pants—her favorites now, because of the elastic waistbands. Was happy with the way they hugged her hips and thighs. And had topped them with a black-and-white print shirt that hung to just below her crotch, allowing her to be able to quickly access the gun at her waist beneath the shirt, while hiding the bulk that was beginning to appear in her midsection. A knee-length black cardigan completed the outfit.

Acknowledging the need to feel attractive, most particularly with Seth coming, she gave herself the allowance to build her confidence where she could. At thirty-eight, she wasn't as young and firm as she'd been at twenty-eight, when he'd known her. And though she wasn't at all flabby or sinking, either, she didn't want to feel frumpy around him.

Part of her needed him to know that what he'd given up had aged well. And because that superficial part of her was able to distract her from the stress, she allowed it some free rein.

She saw his car as soon as she entered the lot. And knew that he'd been waiting for her, since he exited his car right after she pulled into a spot. He met her at the back of her car in black jeans and an off-white sweater that set off his blond hair and brooding blue eyes in a way that was far too delicious.

His hair, always military-short, looked freshly cut. He also looked like his shoulders had filled out in the weeks since she'd seen him. Could just be the sweater.

The moment when she realized she was taking in the sight of him as though hungry for it was the same moment she realized he was looking her over, as well.

"I don't think you've ever been more beautiful." He said the words. She heard them. But barely. They'd been said softly, and were quickly followed by "You hungry?"

"Famished." A state she found herself in more often than not.

He was right to pretend they hadn't had their moment back there. Because it had meant nothing. A burp from the past.

Seconds that had needed to escape and were now gone.

He talked about a couple of his cases while they waited for dinner, giving overview basics that he was free to discuss. She outlined a few things her detectives were working on as they ate, one of which was another burglary, leaving out any details that would put the investigation at risk. Money and video games had been stolen, but Emilio hadn't been anywhere near the vicinity.

"We were right to believe in him," she said, smiling over at him. They'd done something good together.

When he smiled back, and she lost her appetite to the flood of warmth that filled her, she added shared smiles to the list of Seth-related dangers.

As long as she was aware of them, knew where and what they were, wore her protective shell against them at all times, the dangers posed no threat.

She knew herself. Knew him.

And promised herself that they'd be just fine.

Chapter Fourteen

The second Seth walked into Annie's house, he became no man in no man's land. The home wasn't his, and yet it felt like home. Some of the furniture, a chair and table in the living room, the bedroom set in the spare room, the desk in the office, had been in their former home together.

He recognized her mother's china hutch in a corner of the kitchen. He didn't go inside Annie's room, but saw a rocking chair in the corner of the master suite from the doorway as she pointed out her space. She'd had it in her room as a little girl. Would it be in the babies' room next?

If a girl was born, would that chair watch over her growing up as it had Annie's?

Where in the hell the fanciful thoughts came from, he didn't know. Left them to no man, the guy who would be gone forever in a matter of hours.

The tour of her place ended in the kitchen. She started to show him where things were, but he put his hand on the pull of the drawer next to the dishwasher, and said, "Silverware." He reached for the cupboard directly above that and said, "Glasses," tugging it open to reveal his accuracy.

He knew how she kept her kitchen. He'd lived for several years in the house she'd set up for the two of them.

Their gazes met, and he was inclined to linger there, the time-out-of-time element so fresh in his mind, but she broke off the contact almost immediately, turning away as she said, "Help yourself to anything that's here, Seth. Please. Make yourself at home, or this is going to get awkward."

So he put his stuff in the room he'd been allotted, heard Annie moving about the place, and debated about just making an early night of it, doing some work on his laptop in his room. But, in the end, he took it out to the living room with him. She'd offered him use of her wireless internet, but he had an adjudicated hotspot and, settling on one end of the couch, signed on.

And tried not to feel so good being there.

But it did feel good.

Damned good.

"You want to watch a movie?" Annie came in from the kitchen with a cup of something hot from which she sipped. She was looking in his direction but didn't seem to quite make eye contact. Her "awkward" comment came back to him and he closed the lid on his laptop.

"Sure," he said. This night was for her. Doing what she needed to ease her cares. "Your choice."

She hadn't changed clothes, other than removing the cardigan sweater and work shoes. Neither had he, though he'd brought some basketball shorts and a T-shirt to change into, his normal evening attire at home.

She settled into the other end of the couch and picked up the remote to click on a popular streaming service. After discussing some choices with him, she named a couple of newer crime adventure releases— and he suggested a documentary that was getting a record number of views. She'd always loved documentaries. And he did, too.

They used to watch them every Sunday evening. And then talk about them, sometimes debating, sometimes agreeing, but always ending up in each other's arms, making love to start the week right.

Making love was out—even if they weren't divorced and apart, no way he'd do anything to upset the delicate goings on inside Annie or risk any pressure that could cause her to lose either one of the babies. But there was no reason they had to pretend they didn't know each other's preferences.

Annie didn't call him on the fact that he'd said their show should be her choice. She chose a documentary about a guy who'd raised tiger cubs, and neither of them said a word as the story unfolded.

He was aware of her, though, every second of the time they shared that couch. In his peripheral vision he'd noticed every time she took a sip from her cup, raised her finger to scratch her cheek, and her head turned in his direction, as well.

When the last episode ended, he couldn't believe how long they'd sat there. And still wasn't ready for bed. She needed her sleep, though, and, he supposed he did, too.

He also had something he'd failed to mention to her yet, not wanting her to get any idea that he was trying to make more of their little sojourn than was there. But as they both stood, and he headed toward the hall first, he turned to say, "I took off the rest of the week. Dr. Miller said it'll likely be two or three days before we hear anything, and I wanted to be available. I'm planning to check into a hotel tomorrow and get some golfing in."

Marie Cove had an exclusive, very elite, highly rated course, and he'd arranged access through the commander of the base.

He'd golf, too, but the outing was more of a cover than anything else. He wasn't leaving town until he knew that Annie had made it through the danger zone following the procedure. The risk of losing the babies was small—but they were facing two aggravators: Annie's age and the multiple pregnancy.

"I'm planning to work tomorrow after the appointment, and Thursday," she said, as though his announcement had been little more than a normal sharing of schedules. Liking the sense of normalcy, he went with it, told her good-night and headed down the hall.

Before he got to the door, though, he stopped and turned.

Quickly enough that he caught her watching him from the end of the hall. "I'm sleeping in shorts and leaving my door open," he told her. "You wake up in the night, I'm here. We can sit out front and watch another show."

She nodded, but he got the sense that it was a polite response, not something she was taking seriously or would take him up on.

"I mean it, Annie. It's why I'm here instead of in a hotel."

She didn't respond at all that time. Just stood there, looking at him, as though assessing him for threat. Or wondering how sincere he was in the offer?

He'd blown her trust in him.

He'd thought that fact had been driven as deep as it could get before their divorce had even been final But no. The pain from his lapse bore a bit deeper as he stood there, frustrated at the limitations on his ability to help her. In the olden days he'd have gone to bed with her, pulled her up against him and held her securely in his arms all night long.

"We did good tonight," he said softly. Not pleading. But closer than he'd have liked. "It'll work just the same at two or three in the morning. The couch is there. The shows are on."

She didn't come any closer, but was looking him in the eye as she nodded.

"If I hear you up, I'm going in to turn on the television. You can join me or not."

Her last nod was accompanied by an easing of her features. Not quite a smile. A little more serious. But an expression that conveyed her acquiescence.

With that, he went to bed.

No way Annie was getting up in the night, not even to pee. She'd hold it. Lying in the dark, she willed herself to sleep. And, instead, just kept thinking about Seth in the next room. She'd never have thought they'd be sleeping in the same house again. Not for any reason.

Having him close…all evening…with the understanding that it was just a moment out of time…she'd just relaxed. She'd just flowed with him in her space, as she knew so well how to do.

There'd been no questions, no recriminations,

comparisons, or even longings. They'd just…been. And it had been so nice.

So. Nice.

Because no matter what had happened to their marriage, or how their life goals had stopped fitting, she liked him.

Truly liked him.

Enjoyed his personality.

And, she knew him. She'd recognized his laugh when it had burst out of him during a scene they'd been watching. Had even known when he'd laughed. She knew what triggered him.

And that was…nice, too.

She had to sleep. Was planning to head into the station after the procedure—as much for the distraction as the amount of work piled up on her desk waiting for her. And she also had to be alert for the monthly meeting with the brass that was scheduled at the end of her shift on Wednesday.

Turning over, she lay on her stomach, figuring she wouldn't be able to do so much longer. And thought about Seth sleeping not far away. Lying in the bed she'd made for him. In the shorts he'd described. He'd always slept in the nude when she'd known him.

But maybe that had been because of her.

His body had been rock-hard, and a comfortable pillow at the same time. How exactly had that worked?

She knew one thing that had worked perfectly,

every time. The way his hands had moved on her. All over her. She hadn't been with a man before or since who'd been able to turn her on as he had. She could go and go and go with him. Multiple climaxes, and still not come down. Not if he was playing with her.

It hadn't all been the same thing. Maybe that was what made his lovemaking different. She'd never known where or how he was going to touch to set her off. Their physical life together had never settled into a routine. He did this, she did that. She liked this, he liked that. Making love with Seth had been like a new adventure every time.

And yet…when he'd slid home inside her… She shivered, just thinking about it, remembering so acutely how that had felt. He'd been familiar. Fitting perfectly.

Right.

Hers.

A part of her.

Exquisite.

And now her panties were damp.

Turning again, she tried her right side, in a fetal position, hugging a pillow to her breast and abdomen, half straddling it until the ache between her legs subsided a little.

And she wondered what Seth had thought of her home. And what his place looked like. He'd always done his share of housework. Had picked up after himself, and had helped with dusting and vacuuming, too. And dishes.

She'd always done the bathrooms, though. As she lay there, she couldn't remember why that was. Did he do them now?

Or did he have someone who came in to do his cleaning?

At his rank, with his salary, he could certainly afford to hire it done. When she realized she was starting to feel a bit envious of any woman who got to be in his space, touching his things, she turned over again. Those types of thoughts were the result of exhaustion. Period.

In the fetal position on her left side now, pillow shoved aside, she thought about the procedure coming up in a matter of hours. She'd had a very serious, firm talk with herself regarding the actual test. She wasn't to think about the physical particulars, as that would just make it bigger in her mind than was healthy. Her part was to lie where she was told, how she was told, keep her eyes closed, and wait. The parts others had in the process were outside of her control and therefore none of her business. So... she thought about Seth being there with her. Maybe holding her hand as he had for those few brief seconds in the ultrasound room.

He'd been in his navy whites earlier that day, but would most likely be in jeans and a button-down shirt tomorrow as he was planning a golfing vacation.

She wanted to believe his staying in town was more than that, though she fully accepted that the outing was the truth he was choosing to go with for himself.

Underneath, though, she hoped he was staying in town so he could be around for the test results. In the event that something came up, that something had to be done, medically speaking, to tend to the fetuses, he'd be close.

That mattered.

No judgment. No way to even ask the right and wrong of it.

It mattered to her that he be close for that particular revelation.

To emphasize the point, she flopped over onto her back, pulling the extra pillow back up to shove it behind her head and shoulders. Propping her up just a tad. The position felt comfortable. Relaxing and...

"Annie?" Seth called out softly, with a slight tap on her closed but not latched door. Did he need something?

Or have to go for some reason?

"Yeah?" In the tank top and panties she normally wore to bed, she pulled the covers up to her shoulders, her arms on top of them, holding them securely in place.

The door pushed open, revealing the most gorgeous man she'd ever known, standing in her bedroom doorway. His shorts were cotton, dark, though she couldn't distinguish an exact color in the gloom. The T-shirt loose and white—no writing or emblem on it. Just blank. Like something that might go under a dress shirt, except baggier.

It wasn't baggy at the shoulders. Or the upper arms, either. It hugged muscles that had grown since she'd last seen them bare. And they'd been impressively sized back then.

He was holding a pillow and the comforter off his bed.

"Come on," he said. "Let's get you out of here."

"What?"

"Come on," he said, moving his head in a sideways nod, indicating the hallway. "You aren't sleeping in here. I've been listening to you toss and turn…"

Seriously? He could hear her covers move? What had he been doing, standing there with his ear pressed to the crack she'd left in her door?

Why hadn't she shut it all the way?

So, yeah, she was used to sleeping with it open. When you lived alone, there was no reason not to. Besides, she liked to be able to hear the rest of the house at night, usually being the only one in residence to protect it.

"You heard me tossing and turning?" She wasn't getting up, but she wasn't clutching the covers as tightly, either. Truth was, she wanted to go with him.

She just wasn't giving herself permission to move.

"Your headboard bumps the wall when you move," he said.

No, it didn't. She hadn't heard it.

But she pushed herself up on one elbow. And heard the light tap as a brass filial touched drywall. Not a bump, really. Just a…little tap. Something she'd grown so used to over the years she hadn't noticed it anymore.

But when she was listening, she recognized it.

"Come on," he said for a third time. "You'll get more sleep out on the couch than lying in here. I'm going to make up a bed for you…" He turned and left.

Had he not been in her house, she'd have been on the couch already. Because when she was most stressed or worried, the couch appeared to be less threatening than a bed that seemed to demand sleep. She had no good reason for that.

But it was something Seth knew about her. Had remembered.

And there he was, doing something about it. Taking action.

Having her back.

Without another word, she threw back her covers, pulled a pair of cotton pajama pants on, and followed him down the hall.

Damp panties and all.

Chapter Fifteen

"You want the TV on or off?" Seth was already settled in the armchair, his feet propped up on the footrest in front of it, a throw pillow propping his head, when Annie joined him.

"There's a blanket in that..." She motioned to the trunk in front of the couch, but stopped before actually telling him where the covering was stored.

Remembering that he generally slept without covers when he had garments on his body?

Fluffing the pillow he'd placed up against the arm of the couch, she lay down and covered up. But not before he'd seen the more than slight swelling of her lower belly. To a stranger on the street, she'd probably just look like any other woman her age filling out a bit as she aged, but to Seth…Annie was very clearly pregnant.

The evidence of that growing belly, more so even than the images on the ultrasound screen, slammed it all home to him.

The embryos he and Annie had made together were really growing inside her. They weren't just implanting, biology hanging out; they were becoming little people.

He'd turned a small light on in the kitchen, over the stove, so he could see to make her bed and so she didn't trip on her way out, and wished he'd thought to turn it out. Nightlights didn't bother Annie, or him, either, but the soft glow from around the corner was just enough for him to see that her eyes were closed.

And to notice that her lips had relaxed. She no longer had even a hint of the pinched look about her he'd seen when he'd approached her at the restaurant earlier that evening.

But her breathing…he could see the rise and fall of the covers, too, and the rhythm was slowing. Or her breathing was deepening.

He gave her another fifteen minutes. Closed his own eyes, but didn't fight it when they popped open again almost immediately. He allowed his gaze to peruse the room he'd been in for most of the evening. Thinking about how much her arrangement and decor had in common with his. How far the couch was positioned away from the entertainment center along the longest wall. The style of the entertainment center. He'd been awarded the one they'd had in the divorce.

She'd purchased one noticeably similar to it...

Her breathing still hadn't settled.

"I'm awake if you want to talk."

She didn't respond. He looked about some more. Tried again to close his eyes. With a few more seconds of success.

"Thank you for being here." Her words were soft, sleepy-sounding. As though she was drifting off again? He hoped so.

For both their sakes.

"You're welcome." His response was just as soft, a low buzz to send her off to sleep.

"I mean it, Seth. Seriously. For so many years I lived with this sense that I didn't have to do anything alone. Knowing instinctively that you'd always be at my back. When I lost that... I didn't think I'd ever know that feeling again. But tonight...you knew I wasn't sleeping. No one else would ever have known that."

He disagreed with her. The banging of her headboard on the wall—though maybe it was more of a slight tap that he'd have missed if he hadn't been listening...

Or wouldn't have known the movement meant that she was awake rather than just jostling in her sleep. Annie didn't jostle. Once she went to sleep, she didn't move.

He could think about her sleep habits. Or he could face head-on the pseudo jab she'd just sent in his direction.

One he deserved.

"I'm sorry, Annie." More so than she'd ever know. And that sorrow seemed to be increasing by the day.

"I didn't mean that as criticism, Seth. I'm truly thankful you're here. Deeply thankful. That's what I was trying to tell you. You being here tonight…it matters. A lot. That's all."

Jutting out his chin—maybe so it didn't tremble— he nodded. Folded his hands over his stomach and closed his eyes again.

Then he said, "I never meant for you to do it alone." His eyes were open again, focused on the drawn curtains across from him, making out a faint glow of the house light outside her front door. "I came back the next morning, expecting for us to work things out together, to figure things out together, and you were gone."

When she sat up, turned to face him, the covers dropping to her waist, he wished he'd kept his mouth shut.

He'd just wanted her to know that while he hadn't been able to be married to her, he'd still planned to help her in every way he could.

"I figured we'd…continue on as husband and

wife until you were out of school at least…" Though hearing the words then, he didn't see how he'd have thought that would have worked. "It's not that I didn't want you to be a cop. I just knew the marriage wasn't going to work when you became one. But even then… I figured we'd at least be friends…"

Forever.

Because they'd been…*them*.

"Seriously?" Her jaw dropped and he saw the widening of her eyes even in the gloom. "How exactly was that going to work, Seth? I was just going to trot along happily if you took up with someone else? Someone who, like you, had a career that wasn't on the front line?"

She didn't spew anger. Or spew at all.

But she came closer than she ever had before. She'd been so calm the night after she'd come home from the months-long deployment to face what they both knew had been building during their computer chats while she was gone.

And the next morning, when he'd figured they'd both get their emotions out and then be able to figure out a plan for the future, he'd come home to find her…moved out.

"I wasn't taking up with someone else."

"You went to her that night."

She'd called. He'd answered. She'd hung up without saying a word…

"I heard her voice in the background, talking to Coco?"

The dog. He'd forgotten there'd been one. Could hardly remember the woman's name. But he knew one thing.

"I stopped by her place, thinking I'd talk things over with her, maybe get some perspective, but when she made it clear that she thought the way was clear for the two of us… I left."

Silence met his pronouncement, while he sat there reeling with the knowledge that Annie had known he'd left her to run to another woman.

Didn't seem to matter at all that he hadn't had sex once he'd gotten there. He'd already been unfaithful to her just by going.

The pain she had to have felt hit him with a force he could barely withstand. With only one small comfort to offset it.

"I'm assuming Brian was there to help you move out." She'd cleaned so much out in such little time that she had to have had help. Brian, a petty officer to her lower recruit ranking, seemed like the obvious choice. She'd been mentioning her superior more and more in their chats, as she tried to help Seth see how important law enforcement work had become to her—particularly in her ability to interrogate and get the truth out of key players. It was her manner, she'd told him Brian had kept saying, an innate knack she had to get people to trust her, and to work within that trust, rather than abusing it, while getting them to confess...

Or some such thing.

"Brian was deployed again right after we got back," she said. "We've been in touch on and off over the years, but I haven't seen him since we disembarked in San Diego..."

"You told me you kissed him." And a part of him died every single time he remembered that horrible computer chat—the fact that he could see her and not touch her.

Couldn't kiss her himself.

"I told you he tried to kiss me and I backed away from it," she said.

"You didn't report him."

"Because... I was worried that I'd encouraged him to think that something was building between us. We spent a lot of our free time together."

Yeah.

"And I told you about every bit of it, Seth. You were my husband. I was deeply in love with you in spite of our differences, and while we weren't seeing eye to eye for the first time in our marriage, I never ever thought we'd end..."

He couldn't go there. He was still back a pace or two.

"I asked you if you pushed him away, and you said no."

"I...didn't. I...turned my head and he kissed my

cheek, which is what I told you. He was my friend. I didn't want to hurt him."

Yeah, that was right. He remembered her saying those words. And had been deeply offended that she hadn't wanted to hurt the Brian guy who'd popped up halfway around the world, but she hadn't seemed to worry about hurting Seth who'd been at home waiting for her.

"My lips never touched his, Seth. I told you that. And as I recall, that's when you told me about Deirdra."

Right. Deirdra Livingston. That was her name. She'd been a JAG attorney, too, newly assigned to San Diego. They'd worked a couple of tough cases together. Had gotten to talking…and with both of them having no family to go home to, had gotten into the habit of dining out together.

A lot.

He'd kissed her once. Just leaning in for the cheek, a friendly peck at her ear one night, but she'd turned at the last minute and their lips had touched. For a split second.

Things had been so confusingly wrong between him and Annie, for the first time in all the years they'd been together. They'd had disagreements. Fights even. But there'd always been the underlying sense that all was well.

Until that deployment. Her ability to handle a gun

so well. Her acceptance of an offer to take military police training.

Her special assignment to get information out of a group of women who'd been deemed enemies and were being held onboard a ship...

He'd been losing her for months and hadn't been able to do a damned thing about it. And Deirdra, she'd been like him, working in his field, not wanting to run off and put herself in the line of fire.

"You sounded so happy, doing what you were doing. Confident and...for the first time you had a real passion for something other than..." Him. And their marriage.

"So you thought you'd find a woman who put you first?" For the first time he heard bitterness creep into her tone.

"No, Annie. Until you just said her name, I was having a hard time remembering her," he said, fully aware that the words did nothing to put him in a better light. "I didn't have a solution. That was part of the problem. I couldn't see a way for it to work. And I was afraid. I was watching what I wanted most, our life together, slip away and there was nothing I could do to stop it. I couldn't hide from you how much I worried after you took that assignment. How much it bothered me, you being in danger.

"Every time we talked, you'd rush to reassure me that you were fine. It was like I was a kid and you were mothering me. I hated that. And yet, I woke up every morning with a sense of dread. Any day I could get that call… And all of that was happening with me thinking it was only for a short time. Our relationship…it wasn't me helping you and you helping me. It was me being a drain on you and you being a drain on me. When I could tell myself it was only for a while, I figured we'd get through it. Then, when you started to talk about the fact that you'd finally found your calling, that you wanted to go into law enforcement as soon you got home and were discharged from the navy, no matter what I said, you didn't change your mind. You couldn't. And… I couldn't just turn off all of the dread that raised in me…"

He saw her nod.

And knew that, whether she'd been there when he'd returned home the next day after he'd stormed out on her, whether he'd helped her through school or not, they still would have ended up as they had.

Apart.

Despair crept over him anew.

What was he doing there?

What were *they* doing?

He needed to go.

Sitting there, reliving moments he'd thought far behind him…

A beer was in order. Followed by a trip to the gym. It was open twenty-four hours.

He wanted to crawl on the couch and pull his

pregnant ex-wife into his arms, holding her and their babies and never letting go.

Instead, he sat unmoving, alone in his chair.

Being there for her.

Because he loved her.

Annie fell asleep. And slept well. At some point she was aware of movement down by her feet, needing to scoot over to make room for Seth's legs, but she fell back to sleep without questioning his presence on the other end of the couch. Made better sense for him to lie down, too. Felt good, having him there. Snuggly and secure.

When she awoke again the sun was shining through the still-drawn curtain and Seth was gone. His calves weren't sharing space with hers. His head wasn't propped against the end of the couch. The space he'd occupied was empty.

The house was silent.

Saddest part was, she wasn't all that surprised. The first time he'd disappeared on her, she'd been shocked. Scared. Hadn't had any idea how to cope.

That first time his disappearance had been figurative. She'd been thousands of miles from home. Had called him, excited to tell him that she'd finally figured out who she wanted to be when she grew up—that she'd finally grown up. She'd been expecting him to be proud of her—after all, he came from a law enforcement family and she'd be carrying on the tradition—and instead, he'd frowned at her through the computer screen, thrown up half a dozen reasons why it wasn't a good idea. Several times. Over the course of multiple conversations. He hadn't even wanted to discuss possibilities, let alone get the local college information she'd asked for.

He hadn't offered any support at all.

To the contrary, he'd tried to convince her that the person she'd discovered inside herself wasn't welcome.

Throwing off the comforter, she thought about how Seth had come for her the night before. About how well she'd slept. And was thankful that he'd been there.

While acknowledging that his departure reinforced her certainty that there was no future for the two of them.

She hadn't changed her mind on that, in any case. But reinforcement was a good deterrent to falling by the wayside and getting hurt again.

Or allowing her children to suffer the same.

If Seth was going to be in their lives, she'd have to keep it casual—not let him play a role where they'd count on him for things.

She started down the hall with her arms filled with bedding.

"Sorry, did I wake you?" His voice came out of nowhere. Annie jerked in surprise.

"I was doing my best not to make a sound." He

lifted the bedding away from her. Giving her a clear vision of his wet hair. And bare feet.

"I thought you'd left." There it was. Her lack of trust just starkly out there.

If he was fazed by it, he didn't let it show. His expression friendly and neutral, he said, "I was about to go get some coffee..."

So they weren't going to deal with it, the talk they'd had the night before, or any ramifications that came from it.

But really, why would they? Their past didn't have anything to do with the babies that had them currently in the same sphere.

"We've got about an hour before we have to leave for the clinic," he said, his voice slightly muffled as he entered his room and started making the bed.

She watched him from the hall for a second, and then nodded. "I'll jump in the shower now. And could you bring me back a decaffeinated pumpkin spice latte?" They were in season. And had always been a favorite. She figured, with the morning she was about to have, she could spoil herself a bit.

Besides, she had to show up at the clinic with a full bladder. Something about having the test at fifteen weeks instead of twenty made that necessary.

And... Seth was still there.

Not forever.

But he was there.

And she was glad.

Chapter Sixteen

As it turned out, Seth didn't accompany Annie back to the exam room. With the equipment and the three medical personnel required by the procedure, there hadn't been space for him. He'd waited out in the reception area, instead, alternately trying to deal with email from his phone, sitting and staring into space, and, when the room was empty, walking around looking at wall art that he didn't really see.

Although the actual fluid retrieval only took a couple of minutes, they'd told him to expect Annie to be back about three-quarters of an hour later. He could have gone out and come back. Could have taken a walk. But he hadn't even gone to the men's room. Hadn't wanted to be out of earshot for even a second…just in case.

Afterward, his diligence almost seemed like over-kill. Annie had come through the door with a smile on her face, joking with the nurse who'd shown her out.

She'd told him everything went fine. The needle had stung a little, but that was it. And…she'd be finding out the sex of the babies as part of the test results.

She wasn't experiencing any cramping, but could expect some. Could resume normal activities, though shouldn't overexert. And no sex for a couple of days.

She'd rattled off the instructions to him as he walked her back to the car she'd insisted on driving separately from him.

It was as though she'd been trying to prove to him that she didn't need him.

He took the situation with him out to the golf course, playing solo, giving himself time to just be himself, by himself.

By the time he'd played eighteen holes, he'd worked it out that Annie's independence was for the best. Made it easier for him to float in and out of her life as he played a biological role. Keeping track of the kids. Making sure that there was nothing they needed or lacked.

Maybe meeting up with them some, just so, if anything ever happened to Annie—even just a medical situation that took some recovery time—he wouldn't be a complete stranger to them.

Yeah. It was going to work.

It was all going to work just fine.

He'd put his gear in his car when he'd left her place that morning, but stopped by her house on his way to check into a hotel. Just because he was there, because he wanted to.

And because it wasn't hurting anyone.

He knocked, knowing he should have called first. And fully acknowledging that he hadn't done so because he also knew that she'd have told him not to stop by.

She could still tell him to leave. Wouldn't need to. He wasn't staying.

He just had to see her.

One look and he'd know how she was really doing.

Hearing her on the other side of the door, he stared straight into the peephole. Thought about throwing her a stupid grin, but the door opened before he'd gotten it done.

"I'm heading out to dinner," he said. "Wondered if you'd like to come along…"

That had absolutely not been on his agenda when he'd headed up to the house from his car. He seriously hadn't considered it on the drive over, either.

He'd seen her and the words had come out.

What the hell?

She shook her head, the short blond spikes barely moving. Then asked, "Who else is going to be there?"

He was confused until he remembered that he'd told her he'd arranged a golf weekend. "No one."

She shook her head again. "I've got no-peek chicken in the oven."

One of his favorites. And hers, too. Which would be why she was making it. Not because he was in town.

"You knew I'd stop by?"

"No." In her dark work pants and loose shirt and short jacket, she looked every bit the cop. "But I wanted to be able to offer you something to eat in case you got in touch. To thank you for last night."

He remained outside. "I texted several times today. You don't consider that getting in touch?"

"You were checking on my condition. I told you I was—"

"Fine." He cut her off. If he heard "fine" from her one more time... "I'm beginning to dislike that word."

"It's the truth."

And all that he needed to know. He got the message.

Still didn't like it.

"So, does me standing here count for getting in touch enough to warrant a serving of no-peek chicken?" He looked her in the eye, deadly serious.

She hesitated, and then pulled the door open.

He didn't move forward. "If you don't want me here, or don't think this is a good idea, just say so, Annie. I really did just stop by so I could get a look at you. If you were hurting, I'd see it on your face."

"I have no problem with you being here," she said. "We just need to be careful to not let our history get in the way of the present so that, if the occasion arises, we can be together without tension in front of the kids. And we'd probably be well suited to get some practice at it before they get here…"

She had it all worked out.

He wasn't as pleased with that knowledge as he should have been. Wasn't at all grateful to her for figuring it out for them.

But he stepped inside.

And was glad to be there.

"You really don't have to hang around town until Saturday," Annie told Seth an hour later. They'd had dinner and then he'd insisted on helping her clean up afterward. Somehow, without her being aware, they'd fallen into their old pattern of him rinsing, her loading the dishwasher, him taking out the trash, her wiping the counters…

And when she was wiping the final counter and became aware, she became bothered.

"If anything is wrong, it isn't like I'll need to make any decision immediately. They give you time to consider options." She wouldn't need the time. If the babies were going to suffer and die, she'd have to follow medical advice and terminate a fatal pregnancy. If not, she was having them. They were her miracles. It wasn't up to her to decide exactly what kind of miracle they were going to be. Or how they'd contribute to the world.

"You want me to go? Is my being here causing you more stress?" So like Seth to take it down to the nitty-gritty.

To get right to the point.

And when he was standing there in her kitchen, looking her right in the eye, with that soft warm look in his intent blue gaze, she couldn't lie to him.

"No. Having you around is…helping."

"Then I'll be here."

She nodded. Thought about the night before when the two of them had watched TV and she'd gotten sleepy. Thought about the few small bouts of cramping she'd had—and the anxiety every time she used the restroom, afraid she was going to see spotting.

There hadn't been any. She had no reason to worry.

But she couldn't seem to lose the tension…

"There's no real reason for you to spend money on a hotel," she told him. "We made it work last night, here. The room's there…"

She saw the sharpening in his gaze. Tensed a little more.

Waited.

She wasn't going to put any pressure on him. She didn't want him there out of guilt. It had to be comfortable on both sides. Or not at all.

They weren't a couple anymore. Didn't have to worry about putting the other first.

"You sure you're okay?" He was clearly assessing her as he asked the question.

With the words "I'm fine" on the tip of her tongue, Annie nodded, instead. And said, "I'm just…tense, you know? It's two days of wondering if tragedy is going to strike. You're thankful for each second that passes safely, and then worried about the second that's coming and…"

"I'm good to stay." He jumped in when her words drifted off.

She wanted him to take her into his arms. To hold her close within his strength and make her world right again.

To kiss her until she couldn't think straight.

And settled for leading the way back to the remote control in the living room.

She'd chosen the documentary because it was a legal case involving insider trading and multiple court systems. It was something that would interest them both without hitting anywhere near close to home for either.

She hadn't counted on the main perpetrator getting a divorce, and, after his remarriage, having his ex-wife turn on him. He'd thought he was safe as the woman had to incriminate herself to get him. He hadn't figured on the emotions that sank someone when the person she'd thought to be hers for life suddenly belonged to another.

It was just a show. Not her life. Was someone else's journey. Nothing to do with her. She was the woman who upheld the law, who was sitting on her own couch without cramps or any sign of leakage. The woman whose babies had both been visible and moving inside her that morning. She'd heard both heartbeats. One still stronger than the other, but both there.

She was the woman who was going to know in just two short days if she was having sons, daughters, or one of each.

She was the woman whose ex-husband was seated in the chair just a few feet away. The one who'd remarried after their divorce.

The documentary ended. She wasn't worried about spotting at the moment. She also wasn't ready for bed.

"What's wrong?" He was looking at her. She was staring at the streaming service. Picked up the remote and started scrolling, looking for something lighthearted to watch.

"I'm just not ready for bed yet."

He studied her a moment and then settled back and watched a sitcom rerun with her. At least, his gaze stayed tuned to the television. Hers kept wandering to him.

And the love she'd once felt for him surged, bringing her to the point of tears. It wasn't a new thing. She'd been living with it since shortly after she'd met him. She'd known it was undying then, and more than a decade and a divorce later, it still lived.

But instead of bringing her joy, it tended to bring pain.

Grief.

She'd thought herself on the other side of all that. Thought she'd made it to the point where she could think of him without getting tangled up in emotion.

And maybe she had.

Maybe the stress of the babies and the pregnancy hormones were at fault for her current confusion. Her need to bury her head and cry.

The television quieted and she saw the remote in Seth's hand.

"You want to tell me what's wrong?"

She didn't. Absolutely did not. Her chin trembling, she watched him as long as she could, and then stared at the main screen of the streaming service.

"I'm being ridiculous."

"Okay. Fear, worry, panic, it's all real in the moment."

She should go with that. Let him think she was panicking about the possibility of miscarrying. Earlier in the evening, when she'd been alone preparing dinner, he'd have been right.

In the middle of the night, he might be again.

But...

She shook her head, and then took him head-on. Eye to eye. "You got married again."

His head reared back. And she knew he got it. Had made the connection between the documentary and her current state of mind.

That was what happened when two people loved as deeply as they had. When they let each other in as completely as they had.

And the pain when that trust was broken...

There was just no getting rid of it.

"Sometimes I think I'm silly, being so hurt over a marriage that happened years later. It's not like you were screwing around on me."

And it wasn't like her to talk like that.

"It's just...you know...in all the years since the divorce... I've dated. Good men. Honorable, entertaining, great-looking men..."

His chin clenched, but he didn't stop her mini tirade. And she didn't stop, either.

"I had some good relationships. Had sex. And not one of them..." She had to stop. Tears were clogging her throat and she was not going to let them fall.

He nodded a time or two, his face still tight. She half expected him to get up, get his things, and let himself out.

She wouldn't really blame him if he did. Half hoped he might.

Because what were they doing? What was *she* doing? Falling in love with him all over again?

When they already knew the outcome?

Who did that? Who hurt themselves like that twice?

He didn't leave. And anger rose to clamp down a bit on the grief. She'd learned to welcome it in spurts. To use it for her good.

"I couldn't find anyone who came close to being you, Seth. Who could take the place you'd held in my life. I couldn't find a single man who could come after you. I couldn't bear to think about making those vows with someone else..."

She heard the accusation in her voice. Knew it wasn't fair. And yet, God, it felt good to get it out. To just throw it up and have it outside of her, even if only for a few seconds.

Instead of getting riled up with her, he seemed to calm. He didn't look away, avoid her gaze. Or her accusations.

"I didn't even try to find anyone who could be who you were to me. I was looking for a life partner, but not a soul mate." His tone was unequivocal, but kind. Honesty seemed to shine from his eyes. And though his words hurt her, she made herself listen.

On her way to finding a way to have him in his children's lives. Biologically—and more. Seth was there. Maybe it wouldn't be forever. But he'd given her their embryos. And he'd supported the process every step of the way. Because the babies she was carrying were his, too.

Not legally. But in every way that really mattered.

His children needed to know that about him. To know from what they'd come. To be able to feel proud of him.

"Stella's a sweet woman," Seth finally continued. "Generous. Nurturing. Funny."

She'd asked. She never should have asked.

"And I hurt her, too." His gaze was like sharp razors then, piercing her.

Warning Annie?

"She made a good home for us. Wanted children. She was a teacher, made sense that she'd want a family."

"Seems pretty much a guarantee," she said, not completely kindly. "A safe choice. Not someone who'd suddenly find out what her passion was and head off to the shooting range."

It was exactly what she'd done, how it had happened, but there had been times when she was at the range, during her training in the police academy, that she'd thought of Seth. Wondered if he'd have been impressed. Proud of her.

"No, but like you, she needed things from me that I couldn't seem to produce."

"You didn't have to produce anything for me,

Seth. All you had to do was love me enough to support my choice."

Because that was what love did.

And he hadn't had enough of it to give her.

Even more than a decade later, it was hard for her to comprehend that.

"I'm emotionally lacking."

Her heart moved to immediately debunk his statement, while her brain didn't totally disagree with him. Such an odd thing for her—her heart and head to be in such conflict. Generally, one or the other was in the lead and the other followed—depending on circumstance. They were opposites that each had something to contribute to her well-being and worked well together.

"I couldn't take the constant worry. And I couldn't make it go away," he told her.

"Did you even try? It seemed to me that the second I told you what I'd learned about myself, you went on the defensive. And you never let up. Every single time the subject came up you got that way. Pointing out the cons. Arguing your case…"

"I tried."

She paid attention to a tone in his voice. Felt her gaze soften, though her mind was still gunning for him.

"I went to counseling, Annie. While you were deployed. I tried to work through things. I just couldn't get to the other side enough to be okay with you in danger every day. I was going to ruin our marriage."

He went to counseling? The confident, in-control, "so sure of what he could and could not do" Seth Morgan…had gone to counseling?

For her?

"It was the same with Stella," he said.

"You worried about her safety, too?" The woman had been a schoolteacher. Not exactly a job you thought of as dangerous.

So, what was he telling her? That he couldn't handle having anyone close to him? Couldn't have a family of his own? Without torturing himself with the idea that they'd leave for the day and die on him?

Seth shook his head. "She gave me everything," he said. "She needed me to be able to open up emotionally, to give her everything back." He shrugged. Shook his head. "I tried. For two years I tried. I just couldn't do it. She knew it. And eventually my inability to feel what she needed me to feel eroded our marriage."

Our marriage. The words came from Seth. And didn't mean him and Annie. The bullet hit home.

And yet…so did something else.

"You didn't love her."

"I thought I did," Seth admitted.

"You were fond of her."

"Yeah, probably. I guess that's right."

But he'd loved Annie, she realized.

It didn't change things. Not really. Not for the present or future.

But maybe it made the past a little less painful.

Maybe if she'd hung around that night, after he'd told her their marriage needed to end. The night she'd called him and heard Deirdra and Coco in the background...maybe if she'd known he was returning the next morning...maybe if she'd been there, they'd have been able to remain friends.

And maybe...just maybe...they could be that still.

Chapter Seventeen

As far as Seth knew, Annie slept through the entire night. He did, too. He awoke when he heard her rustling around in her suite and soon after that heard her shower start. By the time she made it out to the kitchen, in another of her black-pants-white-shirt-and-long-black-cardigan ensembles, he had her favorite hot cereal and toast made for her. With bananas sliced on the side.

"You didn't have to make breakfast," she told him in lieu of "good morning" or "did you sleep okay?" as she came into the room.

Just like they'd always done it. They'd see each other and it would be as though the conversation just picked up where it left off. As though they hadn't been apart.

"You're working. I'm a man of leisure for a couple of days. Seemed fair that I'd be the one to cook."

In hindsight he saw that he probably should have gone for a coffee and pumpkin latte and minded his own business in terms of eating. Truth was, he had some energy to expend. Being a "man of leisure" didn't suit him.

Not even a little bit.

If he wasn't uncomfortable with the idea of being an hour away in case of a miscarriage, or other bad news, he'd drive home and get some work done in his office. As it was, he had his computer and intended to spend a good part of the day working.

When she sat down at the table, he did, too. Attacked his cereal with an appetite he didn't feel. Did the same with the toast. Managed to finish the cereal.

But couldn't stop from noticing, every time he looked up, that her gun was fully visible where her shirt had fallen away.

Toast in hand, but loath to trust his throat with the dryness, he focused on his life. His role. His next moments.

"I was planning to get some work done in the hotel room," he said aloud. "You mind if I set up here instead?" To punctuate his confidence, he took a bite of the toast.

"Of course not!" She smiled at him. An actual, real smile. Finished off her bananas.

And it took Seth several seconds to be able to swallow the bite of food in his mouth. God, she was beautiful.

And he wanted her.

"I...um...have been thinking..." Annie's tone had him spellbound. "Well, you know...last night after I went to bed...and this morning..."

He got hard.

"...about Randy."

Hell, yes, he was randy.

Randy. She'd been thinking about Randy. Not being randy. Randy. His dad.

"What about him?"

"Have you told him about the babies?" she asked.

"Of course not."

"Well, maybe...you should?"

He stared at her. Then made himself be practical. Shook his head. "That would be kind of cruel, don't you think? 'Hey, Dad, guess what, you're going to be a grandfather. Yeah, Annie's their mother, but, no, you won't be in their lives...'"

"Seth Morgan."

The tone made him hard again. Instantly and painfully. It always had. Every time she'd used it. Not that she knew that. She was calling him out. Telling him he should be ashamed of himself. If she knew the tone made him hard, she'd send the message twice.

He should be ashamed of himself.

And he might be, if he could convince himself wanting her was wrong.

"Do you really think I'd suggest telling him about the babies if I didn't intend to let him be a part of their lives?"

Seth's mind flew from his jeans back to his brain. And pinged his heart on the way. Dropping the toast, he held her gaze. Tried to read her, but wasn't sure he was getting it right.

"He'd want to see you, too, Annie. Not just them. He loves you like his own."

"I know."

He couldn't make sense of it. "You're saying you want us all to be a family?"

"Not…you and I, of course…not married or a couple, but…yeah…with the kids, a family. Is that too much to ask?"

He didn't know. But couldn't immediately dissuade her of the possibility. Legalities cropped up to occupy him. Comfort him. There would need to be contracts. Agreements. To protect both sides.

"I just keep thinking… I grew up with only my mother for family. I'm basically all alone in the world now. I don't want that for my kids. I mean, I have Christa, and other close friends, but it's not the same as family. And your dad… I love him, too. He's a wonderful man who has much to teach them. Just by the way he lives his life. But most important, he'll love his grandchildren and they'll love him. How can I rob them of that richness? That gift?"

He needed time to process. To think. To figure out where he'd be unable to provide the emotional sustenance such a thing would require. To know ahead of time and find a way to prevent his lack from having everything explode around them all.

He needed time.

And so he went in another direction.

"What about the Whitakers? I thought maybe, after your mom died, they'd be at the funeral. Maybe approach you. You're telling me you still have no contact with her family?" He'd found a way to get the question in without seeming completely inappropriate.

And needed to get her on another topic. Desperately. Or as close to desperate as he got.

"My grandmother's been asking for contact, via an attorney. For several years." She shrugged. "I haven't responded. And if they were at Mom's funeral, I didn't know about it."

He heard another tone, one that didn't come from her all that often: doubt. And thoughts of his own predicament fled for the moment. "You want to respond, though? You want to have contact with her?"

"I don't know." Carrying her empty dish to the sink, she rinsed it and her spoon, put them in the dishwasher. Doing the same for his and the toast plate as he carried them over. "Mom was so adamant that they'd only bring confusion and pain to our family. That they were governed by values other than love and loyalty. Money rules them and money doesn't buy happiness. But…the last request for contact from my grandmother was accompanied by a letter several pages long. She said that my grandfather didn't know she'd been trying to see me, that since she lost my mom her life has been an empty shell. She sounds like she's a well of hurt, Seth. Like she's driven by her heart, just as Mom was. But if I contact her, I get into the messy situation of being involved with covert contact, deceiving my grandfather, and worrying about her doing so. About him finding out."

"That's her choice to make, don't you think?" He didn't want to encourage her to enter into a situation that could go horribly wrong.

And yet…second chances…they mattered.

And if Annie could have family behind her…

"I drove by their place a few months ago."

He studied her carefully. Reading what he saw. "So you want to respond to her. To give her a chance."

Turning, she leaned back against the sink. Frowned as she said, "Her letters, they seem so sincere. And if they are—she's hurting, Seth. Really hurting. And filled with a lifetime of regret. Am I as bad as they all were to my mom and dad if I just harden my heart and don't at least give her a chance?"

"I think you already know the answer to that."

She nodded. "I'd die if I couldn't see my babies, and I haven't even met them yet." She rubbed her belly and then said, "But could you please just say it out loud for me so I can see if it rings true?"

She wasn't sure of herself.

"You want to give her that chance."

She nodded. "Yeah. I think I do. But would you be willing to sit in with me…if it happened? Just so she doesn't think I'm doing this all alone and try to push her way in?"

Putting his hands on Annie's shoulders, Seth looked her in the eye. "No way anyone is ever going to push their way in with you, Annie Morgan. Not unless you want them to."

Including him.

It was a fact that allowed him to be there. Helping her. She wasn't going to let him hurt her again.

One more nod, and it was like she'd flipped a switch. Stepping out from his hold, she was all business. Grabbing her things and heading out the door, saying she was going to be late for work.

She thanked him for breakfast, told him to make himself at home, and said she'd bring something home for dinner.

Almost like…they were a couple living together.

Except that he didn't get the kiss goodbye for which he ached.

* * *

Once the decision had been made, Annie knew an internal pressure that wasn't letting up. By mid-morning she'd contacted Clara Whitaker's attorney, telling him that she might be willing to meet with the older woman if certain conditions were met. She wanted the meeting to take place in Marie Cove. At a place of her choosing. At a time of her choosing. And Clara had to be alone, with the exception of her attorney or a licensed, professional safety official.

She wasn't coming at the situation with an open heart or a willingness to offer kindness. She was a police lieutenant and treating the matter from that standpoint. If the meeting didn't go well, she intended to file a restraining order. She was not going to spend the rest of her life hearing from Clara.

Reminding Annie that a part of her life wasn't whole.

She had no control over how others chose to conduct themselves, but she had every right to protect herself and her children.

The no-nonsense attitude carried her through the five minutes between her phone call to the attorney and her callback.

"Mrs. Whitaker said to tell you anyplace, anytime, any conditions."

The hand holding the phone started to shake. Was she really willing to open what could be a horrible Pandora's box? Her life was already in upheaval.

And she'd lived thirty-eight years with the Whitaker portion of her securely contained.

How did a grown woman meet her grandmother for the first time?

They were total strangers. Having only a biological connection.

And yet…she trembled.

Because biology mattered to her. Which was why Seth would always be welcome in the lives of their children.

"Lieutenant?" The attorney's voice sounded far away.

Seth was at the house.

With everything else she had keeping her up at night, she wanted this drama with her grandmother over.

"This afternoon," she blurted. Thinking she'd have the woman come to the police station. Meet in an interrogation room. Until she thought about her detectives and others being witness to her going in and coming out.

She named a restaurant instead. The one she and Seth had met at two days before. She'd call ahead for a window seat. The ocean would be right there on the other side.

And the alcoves provided privacy from other diners.

Not that she intended to eat anything. "Four o'clock," she said. "Have her ask for my table."

She regretted the contact the second she hung up

the phone. Was still shaky. Put a hand on her slightly rounded belly as she pushed speed dial for Seth. He picked up on the first ring, and when he acted like meeting her grandmother at four was not at all alarming, or earth-shattering, either, she started to relax a small bit. She was meeting a stranger with biological ties.

Not changing her life.

She was in complete control of how long she did or didn't stay in this woman's presence. In complete control of whether or not anything further would come of the meeting.

Could just be an hour out of her life that brought no further change.

Seth had sounded...pleased that she'd called. Proud of her.

And that eased her tension.

A fact that she knew was important.

"We didn't reach a conclusion in terms of whether or not to tell your father."

Seth had actually been feeling in control, feeling pretty good about himself, when Annie slapped him with the unresolved topic. He'd just taken the seat next to Annie at the table for four, leaving the seat across from her for Clara Whitaker.

At Annie's request they'd arrived twenty minutes early, just so she could be certain she chose the table. That she was there first.

And maybe, Seth considered, so her grandmother wouldn't have any chance of noticing the small curvature of her lower belly.

Also, partially at Annie's request, he'd been to a clothing store in Marie Cove that afternoon to pick up a pair of dress pants and shirt and tie to go with them. She'd wanted him to appear professional, and yet he hadn't wanted to walk in in uniform. The meeting could be professional, and also personal.

Her arms on the table, she'd looked at him as she mentioned Randy, and then she turned her eyes back to the fingers she'd been studying in between glances toward the door. She was still wearing the long black cardigan over her pants and hip-length full white blouse. As some sort of protection? More chance to hide that she was pregnant? To further cover the gun she was still wearing at her waist? Or because she was cold?

In the past he wouldn't even have wondered. He'd have just known.

He still knew a lot. Could still read her. She had on the ensemble for all three reasons.

He didn't like that the ability hadn't dwindled.

"I haven't come to any conclusions regarding my father," he said. "You know him. He's going to have a million things to say about every aspect of this situation and since we haven't figured it out for ourselves yet, it just seems…premature."

"I don't think we have to have things figured out

before he's in the picture," she said. "He's going to have things to say about his own role. We know, basically, that you're going to play some kind of a part. You're executor of their trust and going to be their legal guardian in the event anything happens to me. They need to know who you are.

"And your dad, it's up to him to determine who he wants to be in their lives. If he wants to know them at all. And as for telling him, I'm the one who gets to make that decision. I was just extending the chance to you in case you wanted it." She'd broached the subject with a whole lot more equanimity that morning. More openness.

It was almost as though she was picking a fight with him. With her all shut off like she was, all sheltered inside her lieutenant persona, he was struggling.

And didn't like being in that position.

Until he realized that she wasn't purposely shutting him out. She was shielding herself against what was to come.

With that understanding, he said, "I'd like to tell him, if that's okay with you. I don't want him to get any wrong ideas about you and me. I'm not going to have him making you uncomfortable with innuendo or pressure about us getting back together. I'll get him to understand that you're open to him being involved, but only as long as he keeps the idea of you and me as a couple out of it."

Her gaze softened for a second as it rested on him.

"Thank you." She nodded, confirming her agreement to his offer. Glanced toward the door. And stiffened.

Seth put a hand between her shoulder blades. Not holding her up. Just...holding. The movement was purely reactionary, but once his fingers felt her warmth, he didn't pull away.

If ever there was a time when she needed him to have her back, it was then.

Chapter Eighteen

The elderly woman didn't stand out as a member of the privileged rich. In a black skirt that hung just below her knees, a gray, button-up tunic-style jacket and black boots, she fit right in with Marie Cove society as she stood at the entryway to the dining room, a pair of sunglasses in her hand and a black purse hanging from her shoulder.

Her hair, a natural-looking silvery gray, was short but styled with little spikes of hair curling down the sides of her face. She could have been anybody.

But the second Annie saw her, she knew the woman was Clara Whitaker.

She'd come alone. Had spoken to the hostess at the podium, but was searching the room on her own.

Annie knew the second she'd seen her. Their gazes met. Held.

Clara's seemed to melt.

Annie had no idea what hers was doing. Throwing daggers? Or showing fear?

As though she'd forgotten there was a hostess to show her to her table, Clara just started walking toward them, her gaze never leaving Annie's face. And as she approached the table, Annie saw the tremble in her chin. The tears in her eyes.

She should have made "no crying" a mandatory stipulation.

This was a meeting. Not a reunion. And there was no guarantee that there'd be a second of its kind.

She didn't stand as Clara approached. She didn't speak, either. She just watched her. And tried to find her professional persona. The one who walked into interrogation rooms to face down violent offenders, determined to get confessions.

She'd never, ever entered one of those rooms with moisture in her eyes.

But…

"You look so much like my mom."

"You look just like her, too, Annie. So much so I can hardly…" Her words broke off as emotion overcame her.

Annie rose then, hugged the woman. Not out of love. Or a sense of family. Just to keep her from causing a scene there at the side of the table.

She wasn't sure why she held on as long as she did. Couldn't justify the action. And gave up trying to do so.

It was a full minute later that she turned to Seth. "This is Lieutenant Commander Seth Morgan. He's an attorney with the Judge Advocate General." She managed to get out the introduction she'd practiced on the way to the restaurant from work. Seth had suggested that they travel together to the meeting.

She'd needed the time to herself.

"Morgan?" Clara asked, giving Seth a watery smile as she held out her hand to him. "Your husband?"

"Ex," Annie and Seth said at the same time. And let the older woman make of that what she would.

An hour later, Annie still wasn't ready to go. They ended up ordering dinner, not stopping at the coffee and decaf tea they'd started with. And Annie had begun to imagine a time when she'd see Clara again. To imagine a life that could include visits from her.

She wouldn't go to the Whitaker mansion. Not while her grandfather continued to maintain that he was always right and Annie's father had not only been worthless but had been the worst thing that happened to Chelsea. But Clara had never agreed that Danny Bolin was as bad as her husband claimed. She'd just thought that Chelsea and her father would eventually make peace. And then, when Danny had died, Chelsea hadn't been willing to even consider ever inviting them back into her life.

As it turned out, Clara had contacted Chelsea many, many times, every year after that, though Annie had never been aware of the communication. Not until she had started receiving it upon her mother's death.

Annie didn't tell Clara about the babies, yet. Their coming together was still too new. And it was better for fewer people to know until she had the amnio results. She just couldn't take the added pressure of everyone worrying on her behalf.

By the time she and Seth parted with Clara at the door of her car, Annie was pretty sure they'd all just been part of a miracle in motion.

She carried the feeling back to the house with her, bits and pieces of conversation from the evening playing haphazardly in her mind. And while she relived the words, she saw something she hadn't completely noticed at the time.

Seth's participation. He'd said the right things at the right time. Been silent for long periods. He'd made sure the waiter was present when needed and had quietly paid the bill before Annie had noticed him doing so.

He'd been there.

And without him, she might have let more months, maybe even years go by just thinking about the idea of responding to Clara's attempts to contact her.

"Thank you," she told him as they entered the house together, Seth having come into the garage from his car parked out in the driveway.

"For what? You handled it all perfectly."

"Only because you pushed me."

They were in the kitchen and she was too wired to head to bed. The next day would very probably bring the results for which they were waiting.

Everything was falling into place.

Or getting ready to fall apart.

"I didn't push you to do anything, Annie. You're the one who brought it up." His tone had a hint of defensiveness.

"You push me to be honest with myself," she said then, not wanting to fight with him. Or have any discord between them at all. "You always have, Seth. It's something I valued in you. Not something bad."

He stopped by the sink, kept his gaze on her as she walked past him.

"You want to watch some TV before bed?" she asked, half afraid he'd say no. Half afraid he wouldn't and should.

He studied her for a long second and then nodded, saying only that he was going to get changed and would be out.

She changed, too. It had been a long day. She felt like she'd lived a lifetime in the past week, and putting on sweats and a loose-fitting, long-sleeved T-shirt seemed like a little piece of heaven.

In basketball shorts and a T-shirt, Seth was already out in the living room by the time she returned. Every time she saw him in a T-shirt, she noticed how big his upper body had grown. And how much it turned her on.

Strong...yet protective. Impossible to miss. And fodder for a sexy photo layout.

A description that fit the whole man.

And one she needed to move away from. Too much was at stake to screw it up.

He was in his chair, scrolling through the streaming service they'd watched the other night. Asked her what she wanted to watch, but she told him to pick. She didn't care. Her mind was racing. In the space of a few short months she'd reconnected with Seth, gotten pregnant, found out she was having twins... and now had a grandmother.

Christa was going to freak when she told her about that one. As it was, her friend was watching over her closely—worried about Seth's presence, she knew—but also about the babies. She stopped down to Annie's office at least three times a day, just to say hello.

She was a great friend. Annie was so lucky to have her.

Seth was still scrolling. She watched him. Soaking him up.

"We're becoming friends," she said aloud. Needing the idea to be more than just in her head.

Remote in hand, he turned his gaze toward her, and she reveled in the attention. As a friend, she had fewer expectations of him than she'd had when she wanted him to be her soul mate and have her back at all times. It could work.

She wanted it to work.

And didn't want him to frown at her. So why was he?

"I don't know that I can ever just see you as a friend, Annie," he said, and it was her turn to stare at the TV, at the list of shows there. She couldn't scroll though, for distraction. He still had control of the remote.

"I love you."

His words hit her like bullets—and she knew, she'd taken one to her vest once. Her reaction was pretty much the same, too. Denial. It couldn't be happening.

Shock.

No idea what to do.

She'd been hit…

"If we're going to make this work, we need honesty between us," he said, and she looked back at him, searing with pain.

And panic.

"We can't…" she said, shaking her head.

His nod confused her. Like…what? He wasn't going to fight for…something? Anything?

"I'm fully aware that we are never going to be who

we were," he said. "I'm not suggesting we try. And I also know that we can't go forward without being honest. You'll get hurt. I will. And most definitely the children will."

The children.

Their children.

The ones they'd dreamed up and created in another lifetime. When their love for each other had been a good thing.

"So...what are we?" She was afraid to ask. Afraid he was backing out on her. Getting ready to pack up and go. To tell her that the meeting with Clara had been too much for him.

"I don't know. I just know that friendship isn't it."

"There are different kinds of friends."

He shook his head again. "You'll never be just a friend to me."

Her mouth dry, she tried to moisten her lips. She had to ask and was petrified of the answer. "So, what am I to you?"

His gaze pierced her with dark heat. "When I figure that out, I'll let you know."

Whoosh. The air went out of her with a force she could physically feel. He wasn't leaving.

But he wasn't staying, either.

He was sitting on the fence.

And fair or not, right or not, she needed more.

"I love you, too." She'd probably known all along.

When she heard him say the words…there'd been no denying the response that had cried out inside her.

His gaze intensified, his nostrils flaring just a bit in the way they did when he was trying to contain his emotions. "That's good to know."

She almost smiled. Was afraid that if she let loose with even that much emotion, everything would come pouring out. Things she didn't want to look at. Know about.

"Who'd have ever thought life would be so complicated?" If they couldn't be a couple, or friends, at least they could talk with total honesty. That had real value.

Deep value.

He shook his head. And then grinned.

"What?" she asked him.

"What you do to me, Annie. You reach out with one hand and pull me in, and push me away with the other."

"I don't mean to."

"I know."

She knew he did. Not because he'd said he was being totally honest, but because she felt exactly what he meant. "You do it to me, too."

"I'm not sorry you came to see me."

"I'm not, either."

"And I'm very not sorry that you're giving life to our embryos."

Tears filled her eyes. She steadied herself until

they dissipated. "I hope we hear good news tomorrow," she said.

"You had very little cramping and no spotting. Tomorrow's the third day, so the risk of miscarriage is almost behind you."

She was trying not to celebrate too early, but she'd been counting the hours. And miscarriage wasn't her only worry. That small baby...

She could still lose it. By miscarriage or stillbirth.

"I'm thirty-eight years old."

And every second of every one of those years was weighing on her as she considered her body's chances to successfully meet the challenge before it. One baby she'd been confident of, but two? And with possible issues?

"The embryos were made from young, healthy eggs."

He was right. And that was good to remember. Her body was thirty-eight, but her eggs in use weren't. That had to be a plus in their favor.

Still, she started to quiver from the inside and then the tears came, racing past the barriers she'd erected against them. It was all just so much. Too much.

She'd never foreseen the path she was on when she'd made the choice to pursue insemination. She'd pictured herself pregnant and peaceful. Alone on the walk, except for Christa appearing from the side of the road now and then.

She should have known better. Couldn't believe she'd actually been that naive…

Tears rolled quietly down her cheeks and she sat there, at their mercy. She wasn't a sobber. Couldn't release huge, racking hiccups that would vomit the tension and pain inside her. All she could do was sit with it.

That was the only way she knew. As she felt the couch sink beside her, a memory came. Of another evening, in the middle of the night. She'd gotten her period. Again. And all of the months of disappointment had been too much for her. She'd lost it. Started to babble about being a failure, ruining their dreams. Not even being able to conceive a child, let alone being a good mother to one.

And Seth had been there. Taking her in his arms, holding her steadily against his chest. And just… doing that. Holding on.

Memory molded into reality and Annie gave in to the comfort being offered. Leaned into Seth, accepting. Comfort. Him. Warmth. Love. She took it all in.

And gave it back out, too. Her arms sliding around him, she was aware of his pain. His struggle. His wish to be something different than he was.

Her tears didn't last all that long. They seldom did.

But when they stopped, she didn't pull back. There might not ever be another time that she could lie against him. They were in their time out of time.

They both knew it. Would expect nothing to come of their taking that moment of comfort.

She didn't speak. Didn't want words to break the spell. Just needed to lie there long enough for them to recharge each other.

They couldn't be a couple. Couldn't be just friends. But they were something that mattered. Something they both needed.

Because of the babies that had brought them back together.

But she suspected it was something more than that.

She and Seth…they'd always had more power together than apart. Like only when they were together could either of them get to fast-charge mode.

Her right hand lay on his chest, an inch from her face. The left was behind him. Her curled fist touching him. Flattening her fingers, she let them spread against his back. Let them hold him to her. To fully experience what could be their last joining, body to body.

No way they could let it happen again. Neither one of them was stupid enough to believe they'd get away with physical contact. Not between the two of them.

Together, Seth's body and hers had always been combustible. His back felt so good. Firm. She knew the shape of his spine, and though she wasn't running her hand along it, she remembered for a second how it would feel if she did. And the dimple in his lower back, two inches above the start of his buttocks. She used to tease him about it because it fit her finger exactly.

She'd told him it was proof that his body had been made just for her.

The thought brought a deep pang. She lay with it. Holding him through it. And wondered if her finger still fit him.

Or if his body had grown out of her when it had grown so much more muscular.

She wouldn't have to move her hand, only one finger, to find out.

And not even all that much. Not noticeably.

One thought poured on top of another and Annie had moved that finger before she'd had any time to consider doing so. And let out a breath when she found her mark. Snuggled into home.

Stupid thing to have matter so much.

And yet it did.

No matter what happened with him, she still had her place.

It took her a second to realize her finger was moving of its own accord. Almost imperceptibly. Loving the spot it had found. Finding haven in it.

And then another few seconds to see the effect her movement was having on Seth. With her head on his chest facing slightly downward, and the light from the TV screen shining on them, she couldn't help but notice a bit of growth down below.

Which quickly expanded into major growth. His penis had always been able to go from relaxed to ready in a blink. Thing was, she had no idea what to do.

Did she ignore what he'd have to realize she'd notice?

Jerk away and make a big awkward moment out of it?

Or did she calmly and gently move her hand from his chest to cover the evidence? Just to acknowledge that it was there, and it was okay.

As his hardness seemed to jump into her hand, she figured she'd made the best choice.

Reactions were accepted between them. All part of being completely honest.

Or so she told herself as she cupped him. She knew exactly what to do. How to move, where to touch, what pressure to use. How to please the tip of him.

How to take away his discomfort.

It wasn't sex. She wasn't allowed to have sex for another day yet.

She was just helping him.

Relieving him.

When his hips lifted upward, into her palm, she knew exactly what he needed. And gave it to him. Shivers shooting through her in the most delicious way as she recognized his sudden groan and covered the tip of him in time to catch his bounty.

Chapter Nineteen

Euphoria gave way to reality and Seth felt an apology on the tip of his tongue. He kept it there. Annie wasn't pulling away from him.

She didn't seem at all sorry.

Using the leg of his shorts he wiped her hand. His underwear and waistband had caught most of the explosion. And he didn't give a rat's ass about being wet down there.

He cared about her.

About finding a them that let him see her. For the babies, yes. But not just for those new little beings they'd created in their youth. For him and her, too. For some kind of "them."

They'd been so filled with themselves a decade before. So certain of their omniscience.

They'd created one hell of a mess for themselves.

And they'd created new life.

He needed to touch her. To stroke her nipples in the way that shot fire down between her legs, made her wet and hungry. To slide a hand down her pants and finger all the right places. He needed to do a hell of a lot more than that.

But he couldn't.

Because she couldn't.

Period.

Not that night. The doctor had said at least two days without sex, but had advised three to be safe.

And after that night…they'd be back to real life.

Whatever it turned out to be. They'd know the results of the amnio. And they'd know if they were having boys or girls or one of each. They'd have reality on their hands.

And not each other's bodies. That much was a given.

But they had the night. A span of hours spent down in the rabbit hole his mother used to read to him about when he was just a little guy.

It didn't take much to move her down with him on the couch, to reach into the trunk by the couch and pull out the blanket she'd said was there, and to settle her against him in a supine position instead of a sitting one.

The task was made easier with her help. No doubt that Annie was a willing participant that night. He turned off the TV and settled down to spend one last night with her in his arms.

A gift he'd never once, in the decade since their divorce, imagined he'd have.

He didn't read a lot into it. They'd been honest with each other. There was a definite level of comfort in that. And maybe it was a plan for their future. They'd design it as they went, with certain things understood, letting the rest bear itself out a day at a time through honest communication.

She'd snuggled against him, fitting into the lines of his body as though she'd never left, her little bulge of a stomach settling partially against his side, and partially on his stomach. He wasn't sure he was going to sleep. Hoped he didn't sleep. He didn't want to lose one moment of their time. But knew she needed her rest.

She was resting for three.

God, let it stay three.

Seth wasn't a praying man, but as he lay there, he started to silently talk to the being that allowed his mother to be taken from him at the hand of a violent criminal. He didn't ask why. He'd long ago accepted that that was a question for which he'd never receive an answer. He didn't ask for anything for himself.

He asked for the health of Annie's family. For special care and watch over the two little fetuses that were sharing her womb...

"We're going to find out if they're boys or girls." Her voice was half muffled by his chest. Her chin dug into him a little as she talked.

He swallowed. Searched for words. Came up short.

Mostly she was going to find out. She was the one who'd be raising them on a daily basis. Having them in her home. Watching as they learned every new thing. Hearing first words. And innocent perceptions. Being there to kiss their pain away. To soothe their hurts.

Things he used to think about.

Things he was starting to crave again, with Annie and their kids. His career had stepped in. Giving him such incredible satisfaction. Challenge. Travel and occasional excitement, too.

Giving him a sense of personal fulfillment that so many never found...

He must be more tired than he thought.

Law enforcement had given Annie that sense of fulfillment.

"Do you hope for two of the same gender or one of each?" She didn't sound any sleepier than she had the last time she'd spoken.

And didn't seem to be traveling far from the one topic, either.

"I'm not letting myself think about it."

She stiffened against him. Relaxed again. "Why not?"

So like her to take that step no one else would dare to with him. Ask him for honesty and then put him on the spot.

He'd put himself on the spot the second he'd told her he wanted to be the baby's guardian.

"I can't take charge of them." There. That hadn't been so hard.

"Why not?"

"Because they're yours."

"Biologically they're yours, too. And you're their legal guardian."

A status that only went into effect if something happened to her. And that was not a mental trip he was going to take that night. He'd traveled it too often in the past.

He wasn't screwing up the hours he'd just stumbled upon.

Which meant he had to think about the gender of the babies she was carrying. To be honest with her.

Truthfully, if they were born healthy, he didn't care. He'd love them the same. And care for and protect them as much as his role would allow.

And some truths didn't need to be shared. Probably wasn't kind to tell a woman worried about her children having abnormalities that he'd love them with rabbit ears.

"I'm going to leave that one to fate," he finally answered.

At which time Annie lifted herself up on his chest, her elbow digging into his rib cage, as she frowned at him. "You call that honesty?" she challenged, just as she'd have done when they were young. "I call it a cop-out."

"It's not!" He heard the exclamation in his tone with a bit of shock. Since when did he get all het up about anything? "I swear," he told her, calming down, thinking he liked it better when her breasts were pressing against him, rather than her arms into him. "I think two of the same gender would be good in a lot of ways. They'll be best friends in all things, going through life's phases in the same ways, in terms of, you know, testosterone or other hormones. And buying for them will be easier, at least to begin with. And birthday cakes and nursery, you know, more feminine colors, or, airplanes and boats…"

Not that little girls wouldn't like airplanes and boats. Annie had done just fine on some of the country's biggest ships…

"But then, I think, with the fact that we're the age we are…that there might be just this one shot…it might be nice for you to have one of each."

For a guy who didn't usually go on much, he'd sure had a lot to say about something he'd claimed to have given no thought to.

He was pretty sure Annie had already reached the conclusion. She had the decency not to say that—or anything else, either.

"What do you want?" he asked a few minutes later. Her breathing was still too shallow for her to be asleep, and he wanted to know. Just so he'd be prepared to support her the next day when they found out.

"I don't care if they come out with green noses," she said. "I just want them to be healthy. And happy."

Seth smiled in the darkness.

He'd gone for rabbit ears. She'd chosen green noses.

Their sentiment was exactly the same.

They were two peas in a pod.

Too bad they'd ripped the pod in two.

Annie awoke before Seth the next morning, sliding off the couch, off him, and tiptoeing back to take a shower.

Reality pouring down on her head.

Their time out of time was done. They'd hear the results and he'd be leaving. Heading back to his solitary life while she resumed hers.

She hadn't miscarried.

Thank God.

She'd touched him. Made love to him in her own way. And he hadn't run off...

And in a matter of hours, she'd know if there was

more to handle than a normal pregnancy required. No more hoping. Or hiding.

She'd know.

And know whether that little one, that weakened heartbeat, belonged to a boy or a girl. And she'd know if both of the babies were free of birth defects.

Knowing their gender made them more real. Bringing huge potential for joy.

And for worry.

In a matter of hours, Seth would be returning to San Diego and the life he had there.

And the only thing she knew for certain about them was that they were going to be honest with each other.

Dressed in blue pants, a white shirt and a blue pullover sweater, she put gel in her hair, ran her fingers through the spikes, and went out to face their future.

Seth wasn't there. His bedroom door had been open when she'd passed. There'd been no sign of him. Hadn't heard him in the adjoining bathroom. But when there was no sign of him in the kitchen, she went back to the bathroom to check. And noticed that his bag was gone.

All of his things were gone.

With a sense of dread, she looked out the bedroom window to where his car had been parked in the driveway, only to see empty cement.

He'd left.

The night, the sex, sleeping with each other on the couch…it had been too much for him. He couldn't do it.

And he'd left.

Because that was what Seth did.

And that was why, though she might love him, she knew not to give him her whole heart. To rely on him. Trying to pretend it wasn't already too late, that she was fine, Annie walked to the kitchen. She was reaching for a pod of decaffeinated tea when she heard a noise in the garage, and then the door opened.

Seth was there in his navy whites, carrying a holder bearing two cups from her favorite coffee shop.

"This is definitely a decaf pumpkin latte morning," he told her, handing her the cup while he dislodged his own from the holder.

Annie tried to thank him, but she had a lump in her throat. Turned so he wouldn't see the sudden tears in her eyes. Took a sip to compose herself and burned her mouth.

She didn't want him to know that she'd thought he'd walked out on her again.

At the same time, she acknowledged that she also believed that it would only be a matter of time before he did so.

They loved each other. In some ways they were very, very good together.

But the problems between them hadn't changed.

Sure, she could quit her job. Find a career that didn't fulfill her. She'd do it, too, to have Seth and the babies and her as a family. But that wouldn't fix the underlying issue.

Because she'd always know that something else could come up, a choice one of the kids made even, and he'd be gone.

Or expect her to let the child go.

Like her grandfather had done.

And was still doing.

No. Seth wasn't selfish. He was just...

Before she could complete the thought, or turn to thank him, her phone rang.

Work. Sleeping with Seth on the couch...she hadn't been able to make herself get up as early as she should have...

"It's the clinic," she said as soon as she saw the screen, and then looked at Seth. His blue gaze held hers for a second, and then glanced toward her phone.

Telling her it was going to be all right.

Or giving her the strength to accept what was to come.

"Hello?"

She listened. Took in the news as a professional. Mentally logging details. She cried a little. Sniffing as she hung up the phone. And saw Seth standing there, his look intent. And his heart in his gaze.

"They're both fine..." Her voice broke on the last

word and she started to cry in earnest. Tears of relief. Of pent-up worry that had just grown and grown and grown. Stepping up to her, as she crumpled toward him, he held her.

And she held him, too. Feeling the trembling in the muscles beneath her hands.

Instinctively knowing that he was far more emotionally involved than he was letting on.

A few minutes later, when she pulled back, she could tell he'd shed a tear or two. His lashes were wet.

The man's heart was all there.

She was beginning to realize it always had been.

"Do you want to know their genders?" she asked.

His grin was huge as he said, "I think you just told me."

She frowned. "What?"

"You said genders, plural!" There was no mistaking the excitement in his voice.

And of course, he was right. "The little one is the boy," she told him, feeling oddly happy about that. Boys seemed to grow easier than girls. In her mind at least. And any son of Seth's…he'd be able to fight whatever life gave him and win.

As would any daughter of hers, she realized, grinning up at the father of her children.

"He tested out just fine," she added. "Dr. Miller said he's already grown enough that she's no longer concerned about him. And now that we know I'm having twins, she's not the least bit concerned about my placenta, either."

All was well.

Seth was still there.

Clara Whitaker was in her life and soon to find out that she was going to be a great-grandmother. Randy would be a wonderful grandfather.

And...

Her phone rang again. Work, for real this time.

And less than thirty seconds later, her entire system changed.

"I have to go," she said, grabbing up her bag, checking that her gun was on her hip where she knew it to be. "DNA just came back on a serial rapist we've been trying to get for months. They brought him in and he's refusing to talk. If we don't get a confession before he lawyers up, all those teenagers are going to have to testify..."

Seth stepped back, his face like stone.

"Seth?"

He shook his head. And just by the set of his chin, she knew.

"Seth."

"You're taking our son and our daughter in to meet with a serial rapist."

She wouldn't be alone. And the suspect would be cuffed.

Didn't mean something couldn't happen. There'd

been disruptions. A table being flipped over, once. But none of that mattered.

Seth had already flipped on her.

"I have to go," she said.

He didn't say a word. Just walked out the door. Got in his car. And left.

Seth made it all the way back to San Diego before he felt much of anything. He went to work though he wasn't due in, as it was a weekend. He caught up on email. Looked through the stuff that had been left on his desk in his absence.

Contacted a couple of clients with updates regarding their cases.

And listened to a voice mail on his office machine from Hunter Bradley, the sailor whose robbery assault charges he'd had dropped. The young man had followed a hunch, tracked down someone he knew he'd seen in the area the night he'd been accused, and managed to find proof that the other person was guilty of the crime. He'd called the police. The sailor was in custody. And Hunter was calling to thank Seth for believing in him. He was also looking for a recommendation as he applied to the military police program.

Seth wrote the recommendation immediately. Sent it off. Called Hunter to tell him he'd done so. And to contact him if he ever needed anything else.

He listened as the younger man sang his praises.

And he hung up with a tight knot in his gut.

He'd been there for a virtual stranger.

And he'd walked out on the love of his life. A second time.

He'd walked out on his own children.

Because...

Emotion built up in him. A sense of helplessness from which he couldn't seem to escape. An overwhelming sadness.

And all he knew was to walk away from it. To move on to something else.

But there was nothing else. Not that mattered. He went home. Unpacked. Changed into sweats, a long-sleeved T-shirt and tennis shoes, and went to the beach. Ran a mile. And then another. Dodging the occasional person who'd opted to spend a December Saturday afternoon by the water.

He ran. And he was honest with himself. More honest than he'd ever dared to be before. When you had nothing left to lose, it wasn't as hard to face facts.

Or maybe facts were his only hope.

He thought of Annie. Of all she'd been to him. And all the more she'd become in the few short months she'd been back in his life.

He ran. And went back further.

When he'd been younger, after his mother's death, and he'd been put in mandatory counseling, his therapist had taught him to try to focus on what was ahead. To focus on the life he had stretching before him. All the good he could do. And all the good that would come to him, too.

He'd have a wife. A family of his own. A career. He'd make worthy contributions to society, just as his mother had done. Because he was her son.

For a time, it had worked.

For a long time.

Until Annie had decided to follow in his mother's footsteps.

Then his life had derailed.

And he'd left the house, looking for what life had ahead for him. He'd gone to Dierdre with the dog Coco and realized that the only life ahead he wanted was the one he'd left behind.

Maybe he and Annie could work something out, he'd thought. Maybe there'd be some other career that could fill her need. He'd known that wasn't the answer. Maybe he could find a way to live with a police officer wife if there wasn't anything else that made her happy. He hadn't seen a way for that to work, either.

Maybe they could divorce and remain close friends, in each other's lives. They could live together while she was going to school, so he could help out with the expenses. He hadn't been making enough to cover two rent payments…

The solution had been a lifeline to him. Hope to hang on to. A possibility of some kind of future with Annie in it.

When he'd returned home to find her gone, he'd thought of her being with Brian, and he'd known for sure that he'd blown it, that she was done with him... Then he'd read the note telling him she was filing for divorce that day and would be making arrangements to get the rest of her things.

He'd walked out then, too. Had looked ahead.

Had eventually seen that them living together as friends had been an impossible dream, anyway. That they'd have ended up even worse enemies, would have prolonged the misery.

And he'd found the contribution he could make to society. He'd become the best damned military lawyer the navy could ever hope to have. He'd found a good life. Self-fulfillment.

But he was forty years old now. And when he looked ahead, all he saw was emptiness.

His wife and children...they were moving on without him.

There was no future to save him this time.

Nothing to ease the hopelessness.

Except...

Going back.

He'd tried that once before, too. Annie hadn't been there. He'd already blown her trust and she'd had nothing left to stay for.

And he'd walked away. Let her go.

He hadn't even tried to talk to her. To tell her he

didn't want to lose her. To ask her to forgive him. To work with him while they figured out the rest of it.

Seth's feet stopped so abruptly sand flew in all directions, stinging his ankles, hitting his face. Spitting grains off his lips, he fell to his butt, wrapping his head in his hands.

He was alone because he'd learned as a kid to deal with pain by running from it. Rather than dealing with it. He was sure that hadn't been the therapist's intention. But it was the lesson he'd taken from those sessions meant to pull him back from the abyss into which he'd sunk when his mom was killed.

And Annie...she'd learned to walk away, too.

The truth hit him so hard he sat up straight. Stared out at the ocean as though words would be written there clearly for him to see.

Yes.

Chelsea Whitaker Bolin had taught her daughter well. By example more than anything. She'd taught her to love fiercely. Loyally. To give her all.

And she'd taught her that when those you loved rejected you and your choices, and you knew who you needed to be—you cut them out of your life.

But it didn't have to be the end. It might end soon. She could get killed on the job. He could be killed in a car accident, too. There was no way to control that.

But this end...it was within his control. He'd walked away from the danger she put herself in once. And it hadn't made him any happier.

Or any better.

The night before, in Annie's arms…he'd been grateful for that one night. And would pretty much give his right arm for one more. Each day of "one more." For as long as they had them. Because one more night had been enough when it was happening. And would always be enough in the present. The trick wasn't to look to the future. It was to live in the moment he was in.

Standing, Seth didn't care about the sand he carried with him as he strode to his car. Didn't care about the seats, or the floors in his home. He was in and out of the shower, dressed in jeans and a sweater, with a few things thrown in a bag and out the door in fifteen minutes.

Annie didn't stick around long.

He didn't have a second to waste.

Annie checked the chicken enchiladas for the third time, pretty sure they'd done all the time they could do. She couldn't wait any longer. She was going to have to pull them out of the oven. Have her dinner, alone. Freeze the rest. And maybe sleep on the couch.

She'd been foolish to think he'd be back so soon.

Or to expect him back at all.

And it was too late for her to go after Seth. She had to work in the morning. Had pulled the weekend shift before she'd known about needing the amniocentesis, and once she'd known about the test, had figured being at her desk would be better for her than sitting home alone.

And she didn't think it prudent, in any event, for a thirty-eight-year old woman who was pregnant with twins and just coming off an amniocentesis to take a road trip alone in the dark on little sleep.

It wasn't like Seth was going to pack up and move from his home overnight.

He had a commission. If nothing else, she could find him in his office—and with her badge and former service, she knew how to ask for permission to get on base.

Monday was her day off. She could drive down then.

Or at least think about doing so.

And think about calling Clara, too, on the private cell number her grandmother had given her. To tell her about the babies. To let her be involved every step of the way, to ease the pain of what she'd missed when her own daughter had been pregnant and giving birth.

Annie was her mother's daughter. And her mother hadn't been perfect.

Annie saw that, now that she'd met Clara. The woman would have been a wonderful grandmother to Annie as a little girl. And a wonderful mother to the daughter who needed her so desperately, too, after Annie's father died.

Sometimes you had to realize that people weren't perfect. And when you loved them, when they were yours, you had to keep working at it, keep trying. You had to find a way to compromise.

And to forgive.

Trust meant that you didn't walk away when things got tough. It meant knowing that when things got tough, they would get better. Somehow. Someday.

Seth had hurt her. Horribly. But he'd come back to find her, too. She just hadn't been there. She'd cut him out of her life as quickly, and completely, as Chelsea had cut off her parents.

She had to get to him.

Enchiladas out of the oven, which she turned off, she reached for the foil, intending to throw the pan as it was in the refrigerator, and head out the door. She could be in San Diego in an hour.

And maybe, if she begged, she could get Seth to drive her home. Could sleep on the way.

Because there was no way she was getting any sleep until she saw him...

She burned herself trying to wrap the foil around the dish. Grabbed a pot holder and heard the front bell ring.

She'd removed her gun when she'd come home, but grabbed it before heading toward the living room. She wasn't expecting anyone.

She was alone.

And it was dark.

Christa had been known to stop by unannounced, but Annie knew her friend was on a date.

One look through the peephole, and she set the gun on the side table.

She'd seen the look in his eye, but it was the satchel on his shoulder that had her crying as she pulled open the door and threw herself in her man's arms.

"I love you," she said. "I don't know how we're going to work through it all, but I know that I'm going to keep trying, every day. I'm going to take the bad with the good, and I'm never going to stop doing everything I can to make it work…" She was babbling and didn't care.

Crying and sniffling and hanging on to him for all she was worth.

She wasn't so far gone, though, that she missed the strength with which Seth's arms wrapped around her. Holding on to her as desperately as she was holding him.

"I can't promise I won't walk away for a moment or two," he whispered into her ear. "But I can promise that I will always come back."

They were simple words. And they were the world.

Gave her the world.

"And I can promise that I will always be here when you do," she said, pulling back to look him straight in the eye. "Though we'll have to figure out just where 'here' is going to be." His job was an hour away. She could apply to the San Diego Police Department, but she might not get her own squad. She might have to go back out on the street.

Tension started to build in her again.

Seth took her hand, led her inside, dropped his bag and pulled her down with him as he sat on the couch.

"I can commute," he said. "I like this house. And I like this town. It's a good place to raise kids. There will be days I work from home, and when I can't, I'll make the drive. People in LA drive an hour back and forth to work every day. And… I was thinking about getting out…"

Shocked, she stared at him.

"Since when? You're career navy."

"Because the navy was my only family," he said. "I've been way too slow on the uptake, Annie, but a whole lot has become clear to me in a very short period of time. A guy looking at the possibility of losing his woman a second time and losing the chance to share in every moment as his kids grow tends to get smart fast. I love the law. I'd be perfectly happy opening a practice right here in Marie Cove."

She couldn't believe he was sitting there. That she wasn't dreaming. It was all so surreal. So hard to accept.

And yet, there he was, filling her with hope and happiness and passion. And sliding her arms around him, she leaned forward and planted her lips against his.

Fully. Openmouthed. Wet. Her tongue urgent in its need to find his. She kissed him without breath. And with a decade's worth of longing.

Her hands knew him. Her limbs knew his. Her body fit into him and she gave herself up to the ecstasy of being in Seth's arms again.

He pulled back when she started to undress him.

"The babies," he said.

"That phone call this morning... Dr. Miller cleared me for sex."

He didn't say a word after that. Not with his voice. Instead, he let his body do the talking. And an hour later, she had no doubts left about how fiercely he loved her.

And no doubts about his sticking around, either.

They were in the kitchen, him in his sleep shorts, her in her underwear and his shirt, dishing up cold enchiladas, when she said, "Just so you know, when you do walk out...you might not get a chance to come back."

He stopped cold, his face ashen, as he looked at her.

"Because I might come after you first."

There was no more cutting off any of her loved ones. Any of her family.

She was in it for good and bad.

For happy and sad.

For easy and hard.

With him.

Forever.

And the way Seth grabbed her up, the tears in his eyes as he kissed her hard, holding her to him, told her better than words that so was he.

The man was going to be around, no matter what.

And so was she.

Because that was what love did.

* * * * *

Don't miss previous books in
The Parent Portal miniseries:

Having the Soldier's Baby
A Baby Affair
Her Motherhood Wish
A Mother's Secrets

WE HOPE YOU ENJOYED
THIS BOOK FROM

HARLEQUIN
SPECIAL
EDITION

Believe in love. Overcome obstacles. Find happiness.

Relate to finding comfort and strength in the
support of loved ones and enjoy the journey
no matter what life throws your way.

6 NEW BOOKS AVAILABLE EVERY MONTH!

#2833 BEFORE SUMMER ENDS
by Susan Mallery

Nissa Lang knows Desmond Stilling is out of her league. He's a CEO, she's a teacher. He's gorgeous, she's...not. So when her house-sitting gig falls through and Desmond offers her a place to stay for the summer, she vows not to reveal how she's felt about him since their first—and only—kiss.

#2834 THE LAST ONE HOME
The Bravos of Valentine Bay • by Christine Rimmer

Ian McNeill has returned to Valentine Bay to meet the biological family he can't remember. Along for the ride is his longtime best friend, single mom Ella Haralson. Will this unexpected reunion turn Ian into a family man in more ways than one?

#2835 AN OFFICER AND A FORTUNE
The Fortunes of Texas: The Hotel Fortune • by Nina Crespo

Captain Collin Waldon is on leave from the military, tending to his ailing father. He's not looking for romantic entanglements—*especially* not with Nicole Fortune, the executive chef of Roja Restaurant in the struggling Hotel Fortune. Yet these two unlikely lovers seem perfect for each other, until Collin's reassignment threatens their newfound bliss...

#2836 THE TWIN PROPOSAL
Lockharts Lost & Found • by Cathy Gillen Thacker

Mackenzie Lockhart just proposed to Griff Montgomery, her best bud since they were kids in foster care. Once Griff gets his well-deserved promotion, they can return to their independent lives. But when they cross the line from friends to lovers, there's no going back. With twins on the way, is this their chance to turn a temporary arrangement into a can't-lose formula for love?

#2837 THE MARINE'S BABY BLUES
The Camdens of Montana • by Victoria Pade

Tanner Camden never thought he'd end up getting a call that he might be a father—or that his ex had died, leaving little Poppy in the care of her sister, Addie Markham. Addie may have always resented him, but with their shared goal of caring for Poppy, they're willing to set aside their differences. Even if allowing their new feelings to bloom means both of them could get hurt when the paternity test results come back...

#2838 THE RANCHER'S FOREVER FAMILY
Texas Cowboys & K-9s • by Sasha Summers

Sergeant Hayden Mitchell's mission—give every canine veteran the perfect forever home. But when it comes to Sierra, a sweet Labrador, Hayden isn't sure Lizzie Vega fits the bill. When a storm leaves her stranded at his ranch, the hardened former military man wonders if Lizzie is the perfect match for Sierra...and him...

**YOU CAN FIND MORE INFORMATION ON UPCOMING HARLEQUIN TITLES,
FREE EXCERPTS AND MORE AT HARLEQUIN.COM.**

HSECNM0421

SPECIAL EXCERPT FROM

HARLEQUIN
SPECIAL EDITION

Nissa Lang knows Desmond Stilling is out of her league. He's a CEO, she's a teacher. He's gorgeous, she's… not. So when her house-sitting gig falls through and Desmond offers her a place to stay for the summer, she vows not to reveal how she's felt about him since their first—and only—kiss.

Read on for a sneak peek at
Before Summer Ends,
by #1 New York Times *bestselling author*
Susan Mallery.

"You're welcome to join me if you'd like. Unless you have plans. It's Saturday, after all."

Plans as in a date? Yeah, not so much these days. In fact, she hadn't been in a serious relationship since she and James had broken up over two years ago.

"I don't date," she blurted before she could stop herself. "I mean, I can, but I don't. Or I haven't been. Um, lately."

She consciously pressed her lips together to stop herself from babbling like an idiot, despite the fact that the damage was done.

"So, dinner?" Desmond asked, rescuing her without commenting on her babbling.

HSEEXP0421

"I'd like that. After I shower. Meet back down here in half an hour?"

"Perfect."

There was an awkward moment when they both tried to go through the kitchen door at the same time. Desmond stepped back and waved her in front of him. She hurried out, then raced up the stairs and practically ran for her bedroom. Once there, she closed the door and leaned against it.

"Talking isn't hard," she whispered to herself. "You've been doing it since you were two. You know how to do this."

But when it came to being around Desmond, knowing and doing were two different things.

Don't miss
Before Summer Ends *by Susan Mallery,*
available May 2021 wherever
Harlequin Special Edition books and ebooks are sold.

Harlequin.com

Get 4 FREE REWARDS!

We'll send you 2 FREE Books plus 2 FREE Mystery Gifts.

Harlequin Special Edition books relate to finding comfort and strength in the support of loved ones and enjoying the journey no matter what life throws your way.

FREE Value Over **$20**

YES! Please send me 2 FREE Harlequin Special Edition novels and my 2 FREE gifts (gifts are worth about $10 retail). After receiving them, if I don't wish to receive any more books, I can return the shipping statement marked "cancel." If I don't cancel, I will receive 6 brand-new novels every month and be billed just $4.99 per book in the U.S. or $5.74 per book in Canada. That's a savings of at least 12% off the cover price! It's quite a bargain! Shipping and handling is just 50¢ per book in the U.S. and $1.25 per book in Canada.* I understand that accepting the 2 free books and gifts places me under no obligation to buy anything. I can always return a shipment and cancel at any time. The free books and gifts are mine to keep no matter what I decide.

235/335 HDN GNMP

Name (please print)

Address   Apt. #

City   State/Province   Zip/Postal Code

Email: Please check this box ☐ if you would like to receive newsletters and promotional emails from Harlequin Enterprises ULC and its affiliates. You can unsubscribe anytime.

Mail to the **Harlequin Reader Service:**
IN U.S.A.: P.O. Box 1341, Buffalo, NY 14240-8531
IN CANADA: P.O. Box 603, Fort Erie, Ontario L2A 5X3

Want to try 2 free books from another series! Call 1-800-873-8635 or visit www.ReaderService.com.

---

*Terms and prices subject to change without notice. Prices do not include sales taxes, which will be charged (if applicable) based on your state or country of residence. Canadian residents will be charged applicable taxes. Offer not valid in Quebec. This offer is limited to one order per household. Books received may not be as shown. Not valid for current subscribers to Harlequin Special Edition books. All orders subject to approval. Credit or debit balances in a customer's account(s) may be offset by any other outstanding balance owed by or to the customer. Please allow 4 to 6 weeks for delivery. Offer available while quantities last.

Your Privacy—Your information is being collected by Harlequin Enterprises ULC, operating as Harlequin Reader Service. For a complete summary of the information we collect, how we use this information and to whom it is disclosed, please visit our privacy notice located at corporate.harlequin.com/privacy-notice. From time to time we may also exchange your personal information with reputable third parties. If you wish to opt out of this sharing of your personal information, please visit readerservice.com/consumerschoice or call 1-800-873-8635. **Notice to California Residents**—Under California law, you have specific rights to control and access your data. For more information on these rights and how to exercise them, visit corporate.harlequin.com/california-privacy.

HSE21R

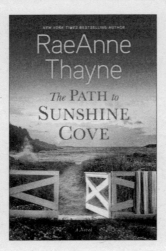